Pride Publishing books by L.M. Somerton

Single Books
Mountain Rescue
Black Dog
The Portrait
Stroke Rate
Chemical Bonds
Testing Lysander
Owned by the Sea

The Wyverns
Mantrap
Deathtrap
Rattrap
Sand Trap
Steel Trap

Tales from The Edge
Reaching the Edge
Living on the Edge
Dancing on the Edge
A Double-Edged Sword
Rough Around the Edges
Scorched Edges
Driven to the Edge
Binding the Edges
Edging Closer

Investigating Love
Rasputin's Kiss
Evil's Embrace
Tarot's Love

Warlocks
Elemental Love
Elemental Hope
Elemental Faith

The Retreat
Serving Him
Trusting Him

Fairground Attractions
Ghost Train
Merry-Go-Round
Helter Skelter

Treasure Trove Antiques
The Lucky Cat
The Gilded Mirror

Anthologies
Racing Hearts: Keeping the Luck
His Rules: Tagging Mackenzie
Hard Evidence: Secret's Hold

Treasure Trove Antiques

THE GILDED MIRROR

L.M. SOMERTON

THE GILDED MIRROR

Dedication

To finding your own hidden treasures.

Chapter One

"Moving apartments involves way too much physical exertion." Landry Carran launched two garbage bags full of bed linen into the spare bedroom before continuing to the kitchen to survey the chaos. "I'm exhausted and I have bruises in unmentionable places. Why aren't cardboard boxes spherical? Corners are evil."

"You're moving one floor down in the same building." Gage Roskam, Landry's boyfriend, poked his head around the door. "And you have half of Seattle PD's finest helping out, so quit whining or I'll spank you in full view of all of them."

"That'd scare the uniform pants off 'em. Something I wouldn't mind seeing one little bit." Landry contemplated the idea of a bunch of semi-naked cops with delight.

"Not so much. I've heard at least three different people say you need a spanking today. None of them seemed bothered about when or where it happened."

"I'm offended!"

"You're a brat."

"I just want boxes marked 'kitchen' to go in the kitchen. Do they not teach reading at the police academy?"

"Not so's you'd notice."

"I never knew I had so much stuff," Landry muttered. "It's like living in one of those anxiety dreams where you know you have to finish something but it's never-ending." He shuddered.

"Are you one of those hoarder types? I think full disclosure should have occurred before I agreed to move in with you, if that's the case." Gage shoved another box of kitchenware onto the already crowded counter.

"You've been living with me for almost six months. You invaded my closet, kept your toothbrush in my bathroom and installed a gun safe in the bedroom. You discovered my rubber ducky fetish, stole an entire box of peanut butter cups and left your huge-ass boots where I'd trip over them. Just because you kept paying rent on your place does not mean we weren't living together."

Gage shrugged. "Your rubber fetish is a lot broader than ducks." His blue eyes twinkled.

"That's where you're going with this?" Landry pouted. "Stop grinning."

"Come here." Gage crooked his finger.

"Nope." Landry folded his arms. "Not gonna."

Gage blinked. "Right now, Landry."

"Or what?"

"Hmm, let me think. There's that new latex hood with the built-in penis gag—that has possibilities.

Chastity for the next week—always fun—or removal of coffee privileges."

Landry decided the three steps into Gage's arms were his best option. He rested his cheek on Gage's chest. "So mean."

"And you love it."

"Not admitting to anything that might prejudice my defense. Ooh, you're so warm and you smell good."

"How can that be when I've been carting boxes and furniture all day?"

"Don't know, don't care, but it's true and that T-shirt shows off your muscles so well. Very distracting. You reduce my productivity." Landry stroked a firm bicep.

"Oh no. You are not prepping the ground for blaming me when you can't find your favorite mug this evening, or if some random object goes missing. Your productivity would increase if you spent less time drinking coffee and more time hauling shit. Less gossiping with Sancha needs to go on that list, too."

"I don't know what you mean." Landry made his eyes big and wide and projected innocent vibes.

"My box of toys is in our bedroom. I have several paddles you haven't met yet. Tonight, you'll pick one then count while I apply it to your ass." Landry gulped and his cock jerked. Gage snuck his hand down the front of Landry's pants to give his shaft a squeeze. "Someone wants that spanking real bad."

"Not me."

"This says different." Gage played a little more. "You're leaking."

"Unhand me, you brute."

"Have you been watching old British films again?"

"Maybe." Landry shoved his groin into Gage's palm.

"*Madre de dios*, put that boy down!" Sancha Hernandez, Gage's partner, shouted from the hallway. "Or at least wait until I have a better view. There's unpacking to do, and I was promised beer and pizza for helping out. I've seen no evidence of either and as I *am* a detective, I'd know."

Landry whimpered as Gage gave him a final squeeze before removing his hand from Landry's pants. "Later, brat." Gage grabbed his cell from the counter. "I'll order the pies before we have a mutiny on our hands. You sort the drinks. I'm not unpacking anything else tonight. The bed's made. I have a toothbrush. I'm set."

"I can't believe you're leaving me all alone for three whole days," Sancha moaned, joining them. "Who's gonna buy my coffee and fill in my paperwork?" Landry sniggered. "I can't believe the captain signed off on your vacation time. Do you have blackmail material on him I don't know about?"

"Pretty sure you'll survive by enlisting some other naïve sucker," Gage muttered before putting in his pizza order.

"Junior detectives are meant to make themselves useful. I'm giving them valuable life experiences and don't forget my garlic prawns," Sancha prompted him.

"And that right there is why I'm glad I don't have to share a car with you tomorrow," Gage said. "There aren't enough air fresheners in the world."

Sancha shrugged. "Lightweight. How are you doing, Landry, sweetie? I hope you haven't been carrying anything too heavy. Moving is hard work, and you need to stay hydrated. Why don't you grab a soda then come sit with me?"

"That sounds so cool. I *am* a little achy." Landry directed his pout at Sancha.

"I'll be on the couch." She smiled at Landry, scowled at Gage then left the kitchen.

"Why doesn't she care if I've been overdoing it?" Gage complained. "I'm the one she spends every day with."

"Duh. Because you have muscles on your muscles whereas I'm a delicate flower."

"Who shifts furniture around all day in an antique store."

"Details. This much cuteness needs to be protected." Landry swept a hand down his body.

"Yes, I'm still here. Sorry. Someone delusional was interrupting me." Gage finished ordering food while Landry got himself a soda. He turned from the fridge to find Gage looming over him. "You give me a crick in the neck when you do that." Landry tilted his head back. "I need a stool or a box or something."

"I think my partner loves you more than me." Gage twisted his fingers through Landry's hair.

"I'm a lovable person. Of course I'm Sancha's favorite. She loves me best because I am way cuter and far more adorable than you. You have this whole broody, menacing thing going on." Landry grinned. "Which is a huge turn on for me, gotta say."

"I know."

"You do, huh?"

"I do."

"I should go talk to Sancha…"

"You should stay right here while I remind you who you belong to."

Landry drew breath to speak but his words were cut off as Gage captured his lips in a demanding kiss. Every submissive gene in Landry's body responded to Gage's dominance. He moaned into the kiss, knees wobbling. Every tug Gage gave his hair sent a miniature bolt of lightning to Landry's cock. When they finally parted, he took a step back, dazed.

"I...that was...wow."

"Now you may go and talk to Sancha."

"Oh I may, may I?" Landry hesitated, wondering if he might get kissed into silence if he talked back. "You don't get to tell me who I can and can't talk to." Gage gave him one of his patented 'don't mess with me' looks. "Okay, sometimes you do. Not all the time, 'cause I'm a grown-up and I make decisions for myself. Like when we have cookies, and I have to choose between chocolate chip and ginger. I can do that."

"No you can't. You always take both."

"Bad example." Landry scuffed the toe of his sneaker on the floor.

"I know you're all grown up, sweetheart, and you're quite capable of making decisions. Mr. Lao wouldn't trust you with Treasure Trove if you weren't. But you're mine and that gives me a say in your life. Sometimes you need a nudge in the right direction is all."

"And that's your job?"

"Along with watching out for you, tying you up, fucking you into the mattress, protecting you from predatory British art thieves..."

"You had to go there."

Gage smirked. "Go keep Sancha company. I'll go wait for the pizza guy and let the others know food is on the way. I think pretty much everything that needs to be, has been moved."

"Bring them all in here, yeah? There's a cooler full of beer behind the couch—unless Sancha has already found it, in which case it may be half-full by now." Landry ambled through to the sitting room, which had a similar layout to the one in his old apartment except for an extra nook for a dining table. He threw himself onto the couch where Sancha was glugging down a bottle of Dubbel Entendre, which Landry had sourced from Sound Brewery in Poulsbo.

"You found the cooler then." Landry leaned into Sancha's side.

"I can scent beer from a mile away, you poor innocent lamb. Of course I found it and damn, this beer is good. Just what I needed. Love the name of this stuff too."

"I couldn't resist it, it's such a cool name." He cracked open his soda. "Thanks for helping out today, I really appreciate it. I know you don't get much free time, and you must have had better things to do than helping me and Gage move."

"How many times have you guys helped us out? Besides, it was this or taking the kids to soccer practice. My loving husband saw fit to remind me that I tend to get over-excited around the coach who I happen to think would have a much more lucrative career as an underwear model. Honestly, he's wasted on a bunch of kids."

"Leering in front of children is not a good plan." Landry slurped his drink.

"Sad but true. However, we're not here to talk about my perversions."

"We're not here to talk about mine, either," Landry cautioned. "Because that would take way too long."

Sancha gave an unladylike snort. "Ain't that the truth? Also, Gage might object. So, tell me what Mr. Lao is up to and why you get to move into his apartment. Gage is hopeless at filling me in. I need to get the details from you. Mr. Lao isn't ill or anything, is he? I kinda like the old guy."

"He's fine. More than fine. He's moving in with his girlfriend."

"He's… Run that by me again."

"He has a girlfriend called Maisie. He met her at his seniors bowling club—that's bowling on grass by the way, not bowling on an alley, and now they're moving in together in some gated community in the 'burbs, complete with health club, tennis courts and on-site restaurant. He's stepping back from the store, to spend more time with her—semi-retirement, I suppose you could call it. I get to be the store manager and one of the perks is to move into Mr. Lao's old apartment, which as you can see has more square footage than mine. The kitchen is bigger and there's a spare bedroom, which is great because I can hide all Gage's junk in there."

"Congratulations! Manager, huh? Does that mean you get a humongous raise?"

"I wish. I agreed to a percentage of the profits on everything I sell on top of my puny salary, plus this place which, despite the lingering scent of incense, is quite a perk. Mr. Lao will still be doing most of the buying while I get to park my butt in the store. He loves traveling around finding great deals and bartering with his pals in the trade. Oh, I also get to look for an assistant. A new me."

"And Gage is moving in with you. That's so sweet."

"I dare you to use the word sweet in front of him. It's practical. He saves a bundle on rent, and I get to jump his bones any time I want. We were as good as living together already, anyway."

"More like he gets to keep a closer eye on you."

"Exactly," Gage said, joining them. "Because someone has a habit of getting into strife when I'm not watching him." He dropped a pile of pizza boxes on the coffee table and the room was soon swarming with all the people who'd been helping out with the move. The noise level and banter grew as the pizza mountain shrank and the beers from the cooler were drunk. Landry laughed at all the jokes Gage's colleagues made about him, noticing that they were a lot more cautious about teasing Sancha. When he mentioned it, she laughed.

"They wouldn't dare. The last time one of them tried to play a trick on me at the precinct, I accidentally stapled his hand."

Landry looked to Gage for confirmation. He nodded. "She did. Not sure it was accidental, though."

"No comment!" Sancha proclaimed.

"Your aim is spot on, and you know it!"

"And on that note, I think it's time that me and this crowd of reprobates cleared out of here and left you two lovebirds alone."

Landry fought back a yawn. "You don't have to go yet."

"It's been a long, hard day and you're going to be really busy with setting up this place until the store reopens on Monday. Take the peace and quiet while you can and besides, Gage is needy. You have to keep stroking his…ego." She snorted with laughter before levering herself off the couch. She gave Gage a kiss on the nose then began ushering everyone out of the apartment.

"Give me a minute," Gage said. "I need to make sure they've really gone."

Landry giggled. He curled into the corner of the couch and nibbled on a leftover slice of pizza. A wave of fatigue washed over him. He'd been so excited about the move, he'd been up since dawn and hadn't slept much the previous night. Snuggling in bed with Gage sounded like a fine way to end the day, even if the bed was still surrounded by boxes.

By the time Gage returned, Landry was half-asleep.

"You have drool coming out of your mouth." Gage's graveled tones pulled Landry from his doze. He rubbed at his mouth with the back of his hand. "So this is how it's going to be. One day living together, and you're already letting yourself go."

"If I had the energy, I'd swat you for that remark," Landry muttered, yawning.

"You look like you're about to go into hibernation."

"That's not a bad idea. Did you know there's a Twitter account that follows a bunch of bears in Alaska and people get to vote on which of them is the fattest before they hibernate. These guys are chonks, let me tell you. They get to eat whatever the hell they like, pile on the weight then snooze away the cold months and when they wake up, they're all skinny. Mind you, I'm not that fond of salmon. I don't think bears eat pizza."

Gage gaped. "I worry about you."

"I know you do. Makes me all gooey inside thinking about it."

"Sometimes I wonder how you survived before you met me."

"I managed just fine." Landry squeaked as Gage scooped him into his arms.

"That's not what your brothers tell me."

"You are way too close to those Viking wannabes and you shouldn't believe a word they say about what I did or didn't get up to as a child. They lie."

"They have photographic evidence."

"Image editing software is a thing, you know. It's all fake, whatever they say." Landry pouted as Gage hauled him into the bedroom. Gage dropped him, and he landed on the bed in a sprawl.

"Get your clothes off, brat." Gage's feral expression sent shivers down Landry's spine. He scrambled out of his clothes with indecent haste, full of renewed energy. "Sure you're not too tired for this?" Gage removed his T-shirt far too slowly for Landry.

"Don't tease me, Gage! And no, I'm not too tired. Raring to go." Landry licked his lips at the sight of Gage's chest. "Your bare skin has magical energy powers."

"Hands and knees." In his rush to get into the position Gage wanted, Landry got too close to the edge of the bed. Gage caught him as he toppled off the side. "Don't want you bruising your backside before I get to it." He manhandled Landry back onto the bed.

"My hero." Landry batted his lashes. He got onto his hands and knees, wiggling his ass in blatant provocation. His cock, hard and aching, bounced. He was hot, feverish with anticipation and when the smack of leather against skin sounded in his ears, he jumped.

"Just testing it against my palm."

Landry twisted, trying to get a look at what 'it' was. The paddle Gage held was rectangular with a tapered end, the handle a snug fit in Gage's hand. "Oh…"

"I was going to let you choose but decided you were too tired to think straight. This is double-layered leather, hand stitched and reinforced with a metal plate."

"I don't need the technical specification, Gage."

"Sir."

"Feeling especially Dommy are you…Sir?" With a happy sigh, Landry rested his head on his folded arms, widened his legs and wiggled his butt a bit more.

"I should gag you." The paddle connected with Landry's backside with a thwack. He moaned. "But then I wouldn't get to hear the noises you make." Gage delivered a further four blows before dropping the paddle on the bed. Landry forced himself to take slow, even breaths while heat, edged with pain, blossomed across his skin. He was desperate to come and on the edge of begging Gage to fuck him. When Gage stroked Landry's sore skin, he whimpered.

"So pink and pretty. You want me in you, don't you? You want me to stuff you full." Landry couldn't summon enough coherence to respond, and when Gage pushed a cool, lubed finger into his ass, Landry sobbed. "So needy. Sucking me in."

Landry worked Gage's finger with his inner muscles, muttering nonsense words under his breath. Gage added a second finger, then a third in quick succession, stretching Landry's channel enough that it burned. "Pl…pl…platypus!" Landry refused to beg. Gage enjoyed it far too much.

"Is that a new safe word?" Gage withdrew his fingers.

"No!" Landry wailed. "Put them back!"

Gage flicked Landry's balls. "What's the plural of platypus?"

"I. Don't. Care."

"I should get my phone and check or perhaps we could find the box with the dictionary in."

Landry sobbed. "I hate you."

"No you don't." When the blunt head of Gage's cock made contact with his pucker, Landry sucked in his breath. "Relax." Gage moved at a leisurely pace.

"I've seen pregnant hippos move faster than you." Landry yelped as Gage reached around his body to pinch a nipple.

"That spanking wasn't punishment enough, was it?" Gage pushed home, then stilled. "I need to think of better disincentives."

"That's a hellishly big word considering what you're supposed to be doing," Landry muttered, trying in vain to push back onto Gage's cock.

"Quiet, brat, or tomorrow you'll be unpacking with a vibrating plug stuck up your rear." Gage took hold of Landry's hips and pounded his ass with unbridled enthusiasm. All Landry could do was brace himself and take it, and that suited him just fine. Now Gage was doing exactly what Landry wanted him to, Landry could relax and enjoy the rush of pleasure, the surge of orgasm, as it flooded through him. When Gage came, he dug his fingers into Landry's hips, yanking him back so that he was as deeply impaled as it was possible to be. He could have come untouched, but it was Gage's firm grip on his cock that tipped him over the edge. Landry cried out, spilling into Gage's hand in a series of uncoordinated jerks before collapsing face down on the bed. For a while, Gage let his weight rest along the length of Landry's body. Landry loved being held down, loved being rendered helpless by a bigger, stronger man. Gage knew it and took full advantage, sinking his teeth into Landry's shoulder.

"Wanna mark me, huh?" Gage didn't bother confirming or denying. He sucked at Landry's skin. "What do you call a hickey surrounded by teeth marks?" Landry wondered.

"I call it mine."

Landry gave a happy sigh. "No one will see it under my shirt."

"I'll know it's there and that's all that matters. Tomorrow, your ass will ache, your shoulder will ache and every twinge will make you think of me."

"I have other things in my head apart from you, you know."

"In that case…" Gage rolled to one side then flipped Landry onto his back. He hooked Landry's legs over his arms, bending him back. "I'd better fuck you again because those other things need to take second place to me."

"You talk a good game, Sir, but there's no way you're hard again yet."

"I don't recall saying what I was going to fuck you with, and by the way, you doubting my powers of recuperation focuses my mind even more on how best to punish you."

"I should be quiet now."

"No, by all means carry on. That hole you're standing in can still get deeper." Gage groped beneath the covers and extracted a sizable dildo.

"You are a virile, masterful Dominant, Sir. I can think up some more positive adjectives, but I need a minute. You're distracting me with that…thing."

Gage grinned. "Nice try. You need more lube?"

"No? Wait, if I say yes does that buy me some time?"

"What do you think?" Gage touched the tip of the toy to Landry's hole then pushed.

Chapter Two

"I'm so glad to be back in the store, Mr. L." Landry fluffed his rainbow-colored, extendable feather duster. "Moving is hard work, and Gage is a slave driver. I'd much rather be here."

"It's good you have a man to keep you in line, Landry. You have a tendency to get distracted."

"How can you say that? Ooh, look, there's a ladybug on the aspidistra." Landry encouraged the insect to walk onto his finger then escorted it from the store. When he returned, Mr. Lao gave a heavy sigh. "Gage has his work cut out with you. I like that boy—don't scare him off."

"That wasn't distraction, that was a humanitarian mission. Ladybugs are cute. I have a pair of ladybug socks somewhere. I also have laser-like focus, and Gage isn't scared of anything. Well, except Sancha. That is one scary woman. She loves me of course."

"Hmm." Mr. Lao sipped his tea, which to Landry smelled of seaweed. "She is formidable. Another fine friend for you, and I know she'll get on with Maisie.

Did you have any inquiries for your old job yet? Maisie is bugging me to take more time off. She wants to take a trip up to Vancouver Island, and I would like to check out a couple antique dealers I know while we're there. Their prices are criminal of course but they love to haggle." He rubbed his hands together.

"Two so far, but neither of them was anywhere close to being suitable. One guy made a crack about my duster being 'way gay'."

Mr. Lao snorted. "I'm surprised you didn't shove that duster right up his jacksy."

"I wouldn't do that to Olga."

"You gave your duster a Russian name?"

"Of course, that place needs an injection of rainbow."

"So, was the other applicant a homophobic asshole too?"

"Mr. L! Your language! No she was sorta okay but Gage came in while she was here and she was drooling...like actual slobber was coming from her mouth. Worse than Bernie the St. Bernard that comes in with that guy that buys mismatched tea sets for his wedding business. She stopped answering my questions because she was too busy ogling Gage's ass...ets. No way was she getting the job." Landry's indignation increased as he thought back to that day. "Over my cold and decomposing corpse."

"If you're letting that hairy great dog in here, make sure he doesn't go near the vintage linens or they'll be coated in fur. Did you tell Gage?"

"Of course. He didn't even notice her but that's so not the point." Landry got a bit fierce with his dusting and dislodged a porcelain horse from its precarious perch on top of a folding, three-tiered cake stand but caught it before it hit the floor. "Whoot! Did you see that?"

"I saw you attempting to destroy my stock."

"I have lightning reflexes!"

"You're more destructive than lightning!"

On the shelf under the cash desk, Landry's cell began to sing the theme tune to *Friends*. "Petey! Kinda odd for him to be calling me this time of day—he should be working. You mind if I get that?"

"Go ahead. You're the store manager now."

Landry rolled his eyes and handed his duster to Mr. Lao before answering the call.

"Petey? You're usually pedaling through traffic at this time on a Monday…wait, are you crying? What's wrong?" The snuffling Landry could hear turned into full-blown sobbing. "Where are you? You're scaring me!" He clutched the edge of the cash desk. "Peter Eustace Templeton, you tell me where you are right now!"

"Is everything okay, Landry?" Mr. Lao gave him a concerned look.

"Petey's crying and he won't say where he is, and I'm terrified he's hurt or something. He cycles like a maniac, he could've been run over!"

"Give me the phone, son. Let me try to get some sense out of him." Hand shaking, Landry passed it over.

"Peter, this is Landry's boss, Mr. Lao. He's having a minor meltdown here in the store and that's not good for business. Tell me where you are, and I'll come fetch you." He listened for a minute then nodded. "Stay right where you are. Landry will call you back in a few minutes, okay?" Mr. Lao disconnected. He ran a hand through his shock of white hair. "I think you need to call your detective, Landry."

"What? Why?" Landry's hysteria was building fast.

"Petey is in an alley at the back of Scorch. He woke up in a dumpster and says he was mugged. He said his head hurts, so I think it's best someone more qualified than me goes to get him. He might need hospital treatment."

"Oh my God! Speed dial 1, Mr. L." Landry needed Mr. Lao to make the call because he was calm and coherent whereas Landry was climbing the walls. He waited for his boss to pass on most of the details before he grabbed his cell.

"Gage, go rescue my friend! Bring him back here, I need to see he's okay."

"Calm down, Landry. Everything's gonna be fine."

"Don't tell me to calm down! I have nothing to be calm about. Petey woke up in a dumpster!"

"I know and if you'll stop yelling at me, Sancha and I will go pick him up right away. We're already heading for the parking lot and we'll make sure the EMTs are there. Sancha is calling Petey, and we'll talk to him the whole time."

"I should come…"

"You should stay right where you are. I'm much closer to Scorch and you have no car. Even if you can borrow one, you are not under any circumstances to drive in your state. Do you understand me?"

"I…"

"Say yes, Sir."

"Yes, Sir," Landry mumbled.

"Let me speak to Mr. Lao." Numb, Landry handed his cell over again. He watched Mr. Lao nod while shooting him stern glances. He pressed the off button then handed the phone back to Landry.

"You get to do what Gage tells you and stay put. He's told me not to let you out the door."

"I should call Petey back."

"You can't. Sancha is keeping him talking, remember? Go clean things — that will keep your mind off Petey...and be careful, don't break anything." Mr. Lao patted his shoulder. "I'll deal with any customers that come in because you're in no fit state to hold down a sensible conversation. You'll end up giving my stock away."

Landry's pout became a smile. "I know you're just trying to make me feel better. You're not as grouchy as everyone says you are. And that hideous jardinière had a much better life as a prop in that play. I haven't given anything else away...recently."

"Who says I'm grouchy? I should sue for libel or misrepresentation."

"I don't think you'd win, Mr. L." Landry scampered down the main aisle then did a nifty side shuffle between two cabinets to escape any possible pursuit. For a guy in his seventies, Mr. Lao could be quite nimble.

"You can run but you can't hide, son."

Landry chuckled. A wave of fondness for his boss washed over him and tears prickled in his eyes. Being called son gave him all the feels and his anxiety for his best friend was only adding to the emotional overload. He pretended to clean for a while, but his efforts were at best half-hearted. His skin itched. He wanted to get back on the phone and demand to know why Gage hadn't messaged him, but deep down he realized he had to give Gage time to get to Petey and give him the help he needed. Landry would just have to keep his fingers and toes crossed that his best friend wasn't badly hurt.

The next two hours crawled by molasses slow, and when Landry checked his messages for the fiftieth time, Mr. Lao prodded him with an early nineteenth-century poker.

"Go to the café and buy some treats. If Gage brings your friend back here, something sugary will be good for him. Get yourself a chamomile tea. It might calm you down. You're going to get an ulcer before you're thirty at this rate."

Landry gaped at his boss. "The only teas I'm interested in are the double ones in latte. Chamomile… Are you crazy? No, don't answer that, you must be, if you think I would ever drink that flower juice. Treats, however… Well, maybe you do occasionally have a half-decent idea."

"I'm going to tell Gage to spank you. If my arthritis wasn't playing up, I'd do it myself. You think perhaps that something soothing would be nice for Petey?"

"Oh… Sorry." Landry was ashamed of himself. "I really am, Mr. L. I'm just…I feel helpless and stressed and…" He took a few gulping breaths while Mr. Lao patted him on the back. "I shouldn't be taking things out on you. I'll bring you back a bear claw." He went to grab his wallet, but Mr. Lao thrust two twenties at him.

"Go! Get out of my hair for ten minutes, you're scaring the customers." Other than the two of them, there hadn't been a single person in the store for the last half-hour. Landry's skepticism must have shown. "Customers on the street can feel the negative vibes you're emitting, and they walk right on by. You want to start earning commission or not?" Mr. Lao shooed him away. "Don't forget my bear claw."

"You're nearly as bossy as Gage, Mr. L." Landry grabbed the bills. "Has he been giving you Landry-handling tips behind my back?"

"I like your man, Landry. We have intelligent conversations about all kinds of interesting topics."

"Oh my God, he has! I've been betrayed." Landry flounced from the store to the sound of Mr. Lao's cackling laughter. There was a line in the café, and he got to the front just as his cell rang. The girl serving knew him, so he listened to Gage and mimed his order at the same time. "Then he's okay? You're sure?" He did his best impression of a grizzly and grinned as the assistant boxed two bear claws.

"As sure as I am that you're in the process of buying baked goods."

"How…?" Landry scanned the café. "How do you know what I'm doing, is there surveillance equipment in here?"

"I'm a detective, not Secret Service. I can hear the coffee machine hissing steam. The one in the café has a particular sound and if you're in there you won't just be getting coffee. Get me a jelly donut."

"Detectives are annoying. Tell me about Petey."

"He has a bump on the head and a possible mild concussion. Whoever mugged him took the package he was delivering and his bike. He doesn't remember anything after hearing scuffling—he was locking his bike before making a delivery to the business next to Scorch."

"So he was in the dumpster all night? Thank goodness it wasn't too cold." Landry had no idea how to mime a donut so did an impression of Gage instead. Jelly donuts were added to his order.

"He was and he's fortunate there was no garbage collection this morning or he could have ended up in the compactor."

Landry thrust money in the general direction of the counter then waved away the change. The assistant deserved it for her mime interpretation skills. He gathered his box of goodies and cardboard tray of drinks, blew a kiss at the server then weaved through the line to the door. "I wish you hadn't told me that 'cause now I'm thinking about that scene in Star Wars where Luke and Han are about to get squished."

"I have no clue what you're talking about. I'm bringing Petey to the store once I spring him from the hospital. We shouldn't be too long."

"He doesn't have insurance, do you need my credit card details? And seriously, you've never seen Star Wars? What is wrong with you?"

"I've heard of it." Gage sounded defensive. "And a nurse pal of Sancha's checked Petey out, so don't worry. Sancha pulled her boy out of the river one time so we have a free pass in the ER."

"Sancha is the best! On our next day off together, we are having a movie marathon. The whole Star Wars series, even the bad ones."

"Fine, as long as there is nudity and snacks."

Landry disconnected, shaking his head and laughing half with relief that Petey wasn't too badly hurt and half at Gage's priorities. He made his way back to Treasure Trove where Mr. Lao helped him with the drinks and food, and Landry caught him up on Gage's call.

When Gage arrived at the store thirty minutes later, Petey in tow, Landry had finished his triple-shot vanilla latte, a brownie and a cherry Danish. Mr. Lao had decanted the chamomile tea for Petey and black coffee for Gage into insulated mugs. He had also confiscated the rest of the pastries, much to Landry's disgust.

"Petey!" Landry dashed down the aisle. Petey ran toward him, and they met in the middle of the store like a couple from a fifties romance movie but with more squealing. "You're okay, right? Gage told me you were but he's protective so might not be telling me the whole truth." Petey rested his head on Landry's shoulder.

"My head hurts, and I have some grazes from where I suppose they tossed me in the dumpster but I'm okay."

"They?"

"Two of them that I saw. I didn't have much time to gather witness information before I hit the asphalt. They need to make that stuff softer."

"They so do! Rubber asphalt should be a thing. I got you a chamomile tea, which was Mr. Lao's idea, not mine, so don't blame me, and I have treats. I didn't eat them all—that's how much I like you. But you're wearing Lycra...ripped Lycra. That's not a good look, Petey, your ass is hanging out of those shorts."

"Is not!"

"Is so!"

Petey twisted around, trying to get a look at his own rear.

"It's just a small tear," Gage reassured him.

Petey clapped both hands over his backside. "I've been walking around like this! I could have been arrested for public indecency."

Landry cackled. "You wear a lot less at Scorch and you were with cops already, remember?"

"So supportive, Lan." Petey sighed. "Can I have my tea?"

Mr. Lao handed over the insulated mug. Petey took off the lid then inhaled the aromatic steam. "So nice...I love this stuff."

"You're a good boy, Petey. You enjoy other teas?" Mr. Lao asked.

"Sure do. I like peppermint and fruity ones and green tea... Coffee is gross."

"I have some special blends from the Chinese grocery store and I get imports from England."

"Wow, we should have a tasting evening Mr. Lao, I found this amazing apple tea from Turkey you'd love."

Landry cleared his throat. "If you could both finish your mutual teagasm, which by the way must qualify as a mental illness, I'll take Petey up to the apartment to change. You can borrow some of my clothes, honey." He handed Mr. Lao his bear claw and Gage his jelly donut from the box of treats, keeping a tight grip on the rest in case Mr. Lao tried to take them away from him again.

"Petey needs someone with him for the next forty-eight hours so they can look out for problems that might come after a head injury," Gage said. "If you notice any changes in his behavior, or if Petey has difficulty concentrating or understanding then we'll have to take him back to the ER. No shenanigans up there you two."

"What can you possibly mean?" Landry grabbed Petey's hand. "Let's go before the mean detective stops us having any fun at all." He towed his friend across the store to the door that led to the back hall and the stairway to the apartments above. Five minutes later, he had Petey installed on the couch, snuggled under a fleecy blanket, sipping his tea.

"I thought you might like to decompress a while then maybe have a soak in the tub," Landry said.

"Stop hovering. I'll be fine once I get some proper rest and get the smell of garbage off me. I can't believe I spent the whole night in a dumpster, so unsanitary. What am I going to do, Landry? I'm not going to make a very good cycle courier without a bike. If I can't work, I won't be able to make rent then I'll be homeless and I'll have to sell my ass on street corners."

"Well, it is a very cute ass."

Petey glared. "I'm serious." His lower lip trembled. "I'm scared."

"Honey, your job sucked. You share a dump of an apartment with three psychos. I think it's time for a career change."

"And what do you suggest I do? I don't have a brain, like you. I scraped through high school. I don't want to flip burgers, not because I think it's beneath me, but because I can burn water."

Landry got under the blanket too. "How do you feel about retail?"

"I don't have any experience." Petey sighed. "I suppose I could become a go-go boy."

"I don't think we're at that point yet. You're great with people. You're patient and friendly, everyone loves you because you have this whole innocent, boy next door vibe going on. Old ladies adore you. All the Doms at Scorch want to take care of you. You'll be perfect for retail."

"But where? I can't see me in some upscale fashion boutique, can you?"

"Uh, no. Here."

"What do you mean?"

"I have a vacancy right here at Treasure Trove Antiques. Mr. Lao is going into semi-retirement, and he's made me the manager. I get to recruit the new me, that is my assistant, which is what I was... Am I making any sense?"

"About as much as you usually do. Are you offering me a job? Here, with you?"

"Yes, and guess what? The job doesn't pay great, but it comes with a free apartment — my old place upstairs."

Petey's hands shook, and he was in danger of dumping the remains of his tea over Landry's crotch. Landry eased the mug from his grip. "You're white as a sheet, is your head hurting?"

"Let me get this right. You're offering me a job and a home, right here with you?"

"Well, you don't get to live here with me and Gage. You have my old apartment in the roof all to yourself. You've been up there so you know how cozy it is. I've only moved down here because, well, you've seen Gage, the man's enormous, he needs more space." Petey started to cry. "Oh my God, I'm sorry! I didn't mean to pressure you or anything. I can just interview more people... But I'd really, really love to be working with my best friend. How perfect would that be? You would be my apprentice."

"I don't know anything about antiques." Petey snuffled.

"You think I did before I started working here? Mr. Lao says it takes a lifetime to learn the trade. He teaches me something new almost every day, but I'm still not allowed to buy stuff. He's going to carry on doing that. You can clean stuff, you'll be great with customers and you can run errands. If we find you a new bike, you can even deliver some of our older customers' purchases."

"You mean it?" Petey chewed on a fingernail.

"I wouldn't tease you about something like this."

"I don't know what to say."

"Yes would be a good place to start."

"Yes! Yes, yes, yes." Petey threw himself into Landry's arms for a hug. "I can't believe such a shitty day has turned out so well after all."

"I love cuddling, Petey, but I'm afraid to say you stink. Let go of me, and I'll go run you a bath. I think you're going to have to simmer in the water for two, three hours, at least."

"Whatever you say, boss."

Landry extracted himself from beneath the blanket. "Do not call me that. If you do, I'll think Mr. Lao is around and don't call me sir, either, because that's Gage, and he has a habit of sneaking up on me in the store because he thinks he's going to catch me doing something I shouldn't and have an excuse to punish me."

"If I'm living above you, am I going to need loud music to drown out your yelling when he spanks you?" Petey blinked.

"How anyone who looks as innocent as you do can be as kinky as you are, I'll never know. I recommend a good set of headphones." Landry ignored Petey's grin and headed for the bathroom. *I really need to find Petey a Dom. The problem is going to be finding one that's good enough for him.*

Chapter Three

"Your couch is really comfy," Petey said from his perch on a stool behind the cash desk in the store. "I slept so well, and my headache is nearly gone."

"It's a couch that hugs and I'm glad your head is better. Hopefully you won't have to sleep on it again, though, because I spoke to my friend Prisha—her dad owns the Eastern Emporium across the street—she has a cousin who has a wholesale bed business. She's sorting a new mattress for the bed frame in your apartment. Gage and I took mine with us because it wasn't that old. Gage splurged on an expensive pillow-top when he started staying over all the time." Landry finished counting the petty cash.

Petey frowned. "I don't have much in the way of savings. Maybe when I've been working here a while."

"Oh honey, after you'd fallen asleep last night, I put the word out to the guys at Scorch that you were moving into a new place and Gage threatened a few of his cop friends. I think you'll be surprised what shows up today to make your place homey."

"I'm not a charity case, Landry. I can save up. It'll take a while but..."

"Housewarming gifts are not charity. If people want to help then you should let them — everyone has stuff they don't need. Gage and I have pooled two places, so we have all kinds of spares. You'll get your chance to pay it forward another time. Now, do you think you can handle the cash register?"

"I think I've got it...I'll yell if I get stuck."

"Don't get your fingers jammed in the drawer. I've been there and I can tell you, I found new levels of cursing that day."

"Ouchies!"

"Are you sure you're okay? You're a bit pale."

"I'm in shock. I got mugged, narrowly avoided death by tentacle-infested trash compactor, found a new home and a new job with my best friend all in the space of twenty-four hours. I need some time to process."

"Fair enough. Ooh, did I tell you Gage has never seen *Stars Wars*?"

"What the...fudge! I mean he's gorgeous and Dommy but why are you with him again?"

"Because he's gorgeous and Dommy?"

"I suppose that does excuse an utter lack of geekery."

"He also does this thing where he spanks me and squeezes my...uh, never mind."

"You can't stop there! I have a head injury. My brain might explode if you don't keep going."

"If it does, you're cleaning up the blobby stuff. I have managerial privileges, and you don't know every scrumptious detail of what Gage and I get up to when we have sexy time." Petey pouted but only managed to look cuter. "Don't look at me like that. When you have a Dom of your own, you'll want to keep the juiciest bits to yourself too." The bell over the door jangled and several customers came inside. "Time to do some actual work. Then we can have a coffee break. I'll even let you drink tea because I'm that nice."

"Okay. Uh, Landry…there's a fire truck out front." Petey pointed at the street.

"I hope nothing's on fire!" Landry jogged over to the door but before he could open it, several firemen pushed their way inside. He spotted a friend he knew from Scorch. "Carson? What's going on? The building isn't alight, is it? I know I cooked Pop-Tarts this morning, but they weren't even charred."

"No need to evacuate. We're on our way to a charity event at Teddy Bear's Kindergarten but Gage told me Petey had a new place here and needed some home comforts. We have some stuff for him…is he here?"

"I am." Petey came to stand at Landry's side. "Hello, Master Carson."

"Just Carson's fine, Petey. We're not at Scorch now."

Petey gasped. "Sorry! Did I just out you to your crew?"

One of Carson's colleagues snorted with laughter. "We all know he's a kinky fucker."

"Which is why I'm in charge, and you'll be cleaning the tender with a toothbrush this evening, Harris. Where do you want all this stuff?" Carson's voice softened when he addressed Petey who had apparently lost the power of speech.

Landry tracked the pair of them like he was watching a game of tennis. "Top floor, Carson. You guys can use the door over there. There's no elevator but you guys like running upstairs, don't you? Good for keeping fit." Landry gestured to the way through to the stairwell. "The apartment door's not locked. Just put the boxes anywhere, Petey hasn't moved in yet, he's been staying with me."

"Got it. You heard him, guys." A procession of men carrying boxes and bags trekked through the store while Petey watched, wide-eyed. Landry grinned and tried not to drool at all the fit firemen. "Well, well, I think you have an admirer."

Petey blushed to the roots of his floppy blond hair. "You're deranged."

"And you're the color of one of those British telephone boxes. You could do worse, you know. Master Carson is a well-respected Dom. He's friends with me and Gage so he has to be the best."

Sighing, Petey rested his chin on his hands, elbows on the cash desk. "He's gorgeous, but he's just being nice. Why would he even give me a second glance? He has subs falling over themselves to play with him at Scorch. He could have anyone."

"I love you, but could you be any denser? Have you looked in the mirror recently? Hot bod, check. Pretty face, check. Aura of vulnerability, check. You're a Dom magnet, my friend. Own it. I'd guess that all you have to do is flutter those golden eyelashes in Carson's direction and you'll have him right where you want him."

"Where I want him would not be appropriate in this store."

Landry giggled. "Well, from the sound of elephants thundering downstairs, I'd guess they're coming back."

The parade of firemen, now empty-handed, made the return journey through the store, much to the delight of a couple of middle-aged ladies browsing the book display. Carson stopped at the cash desk.

"All done. We left a couple lawn chairs but my sister has a couch and armchair she wants rid of because they bought a new suite. I'll bring it over when I have my truck. You need some help settling in, Petey?"

"I... I mean... That would be... If you think... I could..."

"I'll be here at eight. I'll bring take-out and I can help you arrange things how you want them."

"Yes, Sir."

"Good. I'll see you later."

Landry wondered if it was possible for Petey's eyes to get any wider as he watched Carson stroll down the aisle, uniform pants hugging his ass. "You look like a spaniel puppy begging for a treat. Come to think of it, Carson will probably enjoy you begging."

"He's coming here, tonight—to spend time alone with me! What am I going to do, Landry?"

"Be your own, cute, adorable self. I'd guess Carson's already smitten. He saw an opening and walked right through... Typical Dom. He's gonna take what he wants and what he wants is you."

Petey gulped. "Okay, that's freaking me out a little."

"There's no need to be scared. You've played with some hard-core Doms at Scorch, you can handle yourself and Carson is one of the good guys."

"This wouldn't be playing, though, would it?"

"We all have to grow up sometime, and I know how that sounds coming from me, but once I found Gage, I had no interest in playing with anyone else. Find the right Dom, and you're anchored for life and I don't mean like mafia anchored where you're tied to it and lobbed in the ocean. Gage stops me drifting all over the place, psychologically speaking."

Petey beamed, but it wasn't for Landry's benefit. It was the two ladies approaching the cash desk, both holding stacks of books. "Ladies, what a pleasure. I hope you found everything you were looking for," Petey said, turning on the charm.

"Why, aren't you the sweetest? Beryl, I think we are going to be regular customers here. Do you by any chance have a schedule for when the firefighters will be back?"

Landry snorted with laughter. "You have excellent taste ladies. I'll leave you in Petey's capable hands." He headed out to get drinks, content that he was able to stop worrying about his friend. Carson was perfectly qualified to take care of Petey's needs as a submissive, Landry could concentrate on making sure Petey got into mischief.

* * * *

That evening, after a flushed, excited Petey had escorted Carson upstairs to Petey's new home, Landry bopped around his kitchen putting the finishing touches to the pasta dish he was preparing for him and Gage. He expected Gage at any minute and he'd promised to bring pie for dessert. The sauce was done, water boiling ready for the pasta and garlic bread prepped to heat in the oven. Landry didn't want to cook the pasta too soon or they'd go soggy but when he heard Gage coming through the door, he scooped the little bowtie shapes into the water and turned the oven on.

"Dinner will be ready in ten minutes," he called. "Did you remember pie?"

Gage appeared in the kitchen doorway, tie loosened and jacket slung over one arm. "It's good to know where I come in your priorities — somewhere down the list after pie." Landry shimmied over to him for a kiss.

"Welcome home, honey. How was your day? What kind of pie did you bring me?" He gasped as Gage shoved him against the doorframe and grabbed his hands, holding them over Landry's head. Gage kissed him until he was gasping for air and his cock challenging his zipper. "If it helps, you came a really close second to pie."

"Good to know." Gage set him free. "Do I have time for a quick shower before we eat?"

"You are a little stinky," Landry said, breathing deeply. "I like it."

Gage shook his head. "How long?"

"You have ten minutes. Give me my pie so I can put it in the oven to warm. I got some of that vanilla cream you like from the deli to go with it."

"I put it on the table, I'll go fetch it."

Landry stirred his sauce, taking a taste from the spoon. "Perfect."

Gage handed him the pie in a paper bag. "Peach."

"My favorite!" Landry yelled after him as Gage ran for the bathroom.

"I know!" Gage shouted back.

With a happy wiggle, Landry slid the pie from its bag into the oven. He spent a few minutes, while Gage showered, setting the table. Now they had extra space he wanted to make use of it, rather than balancing plates on their laps in front of the TV like they'd had to do in his old apartment. They had little enough time together when they weren't both too tired for anything but sleep, it would be nice to have a chance to sit, eat and chat.

"Wow, look at me getting all domesticated."

"Are you talking to yourself again?" Gage emerged from the direction of their bedroom, pulling a T-shirt over his head. Landry leered.

"No need to cover up on my account."

"You're shameless."

Landry shrugged. "I was just commenting on how domestic we're getting. I like it."

"So do I." Gage grabbed him from behind then started sucking on Landry's neck. "You taste good. You need more of my marks on you."

"Or you could eat the food I made rather than me." Despite his words, Landry made no attempt to escape Gage's hold.

"There's other parts of you I'd like to get my teeth into. Maybe *you* should sit through dinner naked."

"Is that an order, Sir?"

Gage slipped his hands under Landry's shirt, stroked his belly then gave both nipples a pinch. Landry arched his back, moaning. "Feed me, slave boy. I'll consider what to do with you when my belly's full."

"Oh, you're asking for a smacking!" Landry rounded on his lover only to find him grinning from ear to ear. "You're a nightmare. Sit down before you say something that gets you in worse trouble. Slave boy, my ass. If I don't fetch dinner now it's gonna be ruined."

Not seeming chastened in the slightest, Gage took a seat. Landry flounced to the kitchen because after that comment from Gage he deserved to display some righteous indignation. He breathed in the savory aromas and smiled. His stomach rumbled so he hurried to serve the food then made two trips to the table before he collapsed in the chair next to Gage. "I have every admiration for wait staff. Table service is exhausting."

"You've been on your feet in the store all day and training a newbie, I'm not surprised you're flagging. What's this? It smells great."

"Smoked chicken and broccoli pasta, garlic bread and salad."

"Wow, you're spoiling me."

A warm glow lit Landry's body. Praise from Gage was something he longed for and treasured. "My pleasure. I enjoy cooking for you."

"All the better for me." Gage made happy noises as he cleared half his plate without taking a breath. "Coming home to you and this…I could get used to it."

Landry swallowed, his throat a little tight. "You can thank me later when we're horizontal."

"No house guest tonight?"

"Nope. Prisha's cousin came through with a mattress, and I imagine by now, Petey and Carson are probably testing it out."

"Carson Cole, from Scorch?"

"Uh huh. He and half his fire house showed up earlier with a bunch of stuff for Petey. Carson offered to come back tonight and help Petey unpack, though I'm not sure unpacking was what he had on his mind. I think he would have stripped Petey right there in the store and bent him over the nearest flat surface if he could."

"About time he made a move." Gage stabbed a piece of broccoli with his fork. "Carson has had his eye on Petey for a while."

"Why didn't you tell me?" Landry exclaimed.

"Because you would have blabbed to Petey in a heartbeat. Carson's thoughtful, he needed to take his time. I'm glad the guys showed up, though, Carson drummed up a lot of support after I spoke to him."

"Petey really likes him."

"I think they're well suited. Petey's a bit of a pain slut behind that cute exterior, and Carson likes to deliver a sound caning."

"He'll take things slow, though, right? Petey was nervous about spending time with him at home. It's a whole different vibe to playing with a Dom at Scorch."

"He's one of the good guys, love. Petey doesn't have a thing to worry about unless his smoke alarm is out of order, then he might be sitting on a cushion for a while."

"I told Petey the same thing—about him being a good guy, I mean—and you know that alarm works fine—it was mine until a few days ago."

"Petey's ass is a fraction safer then. I'd still have a cushion handy if I were you." Gage belched and pushed his empty plate away. "I left some room for pie. Gonna share?"

"Such a charmer."

"Hey, in some cultures belching is a sign of appreciation."

Landry went to fetch the pie. By the time they were done with dessert, Landry couldn't contemplate moving. "I ate way too much. That pie was epic."

"I'd say that third slice was the deal breaker." Gage cleared the table. When he returned from the kitchen he brought coffee with him. He held the mug under Landry's nose. "Follow me to the couch if you want the coffee."

"So mean." Landry dragged himself up then hauled over to the couch where he collapsed into the corner seat. He waggled his fingers at Gage. "Gimme."

"Demanding brat." Gage handed over the mug. "If I ever want you to follow me somewhere you don't want to go, I'll just waft coffee fumes in your direction." He sat on the couch next to Landry. "Or I suppose I could just use a collar and lead."

Landry spluttered into his coffee. "Note to self, always check destination when getting in a vehicle with detective boyfriend."

Gage laughed. "Drink your coffee so we can snuggle."

Landry clutched his mug but stared at Gage's lap. A pair of strong thighs encased in denim exceeded even coffee in his affections. He put the mug on the floor, then crawled into Gage's lap. Gage held his own mug out of the way while Landry got situated, leaning against his chest.

"So warm." Landry nuzzled against Gage's shoulder. Gage abandoned his own drink in favor of wrapping his arms around Landry. "Just you, me and peace and quiet. I love it. Love you."

"Love you too. And you're right, having our own place together is great. Sancha gave me some serious shit because I wanted to leave work early."

"Oh, because you wanted to get back to me?"

"No, because I was hungry."

Landry smacked Gage's arm. "You'd better be kidding."

"Of course I am." Gage tugged Landry's hair, tilting his head back to get him in position for a long, slow kiss. "We have a shitload of cases at the moment, most of which are going nowhere fast. It's good to have something to look forward to at the end of the day."

"Same. Even though my commute has halved from one minute to thirty seconds, I'm still glad to get away from the store."

"And it was your first day in charge. How did that go?"

"I was a little nervous. Mr. Lao rang me four times, checking up on us."

"Treasure Trove is his baby. He's bound to be a bit anxious until you get into your stride. I know he's left you on your own before, but it wasn't permanent. This is a whole change of lifestyle for him. I guess he'll be clingy for a while."

"I suppose we'll both get used to it."

"Hey, I have something to show you. I got this in the mail at work. You wouldn't think the police department would get junk mail, but we do." Gage pulled a folded piece of paper from his pocket. "It's a flyer for a pop-up flea market that's taking place in the Chinese district on Sunday. I thought we could go."

Landry smoothed the piece of paper against Gage's chest. "Oh, wow. I'd love to. You never know when you might find an unexpected treasure, and Mr. Lao has been teaching me what to look out for. It'll be fun, and there are bound to be food stalls. We can stuff ourselves with junk food while we shop. Now I'm craving hot donuts, straight out of the fryer."

"I'm not sure how you can even contemplate food after what we've just eaten, but it's a date."

"Excellent. I'm excited and my stomach has a superfast recovery time, a bit like your d…"

"Landry…"

"Digestion. I was going to say digestion. You have a one-track mind."

"You were not."

"Was so." Landry didn't dare meet Gage's steely gaze.

"Perhaps we should have a conversation about you always telling your Dom the truth?"

"I'm good at talking," Landry said. "I can do conversation."

"This conversation is going to be between your ass and my hand."

Before Landry realized what was going on, Gage had swung him around so that he was face down over Gage's lap. "Hey! I just ate. There is a good chance I may throw up, just so you know." Gage delivered six hard whacks to Landry's backside before lifting him upright. Landry rubbed at his ass with both hands. "Stop grinning."

"Why? I'm having a good time and I can see you are too." Gage gave Landry's crotch a rub through his pants. A spanking never failed to make Landry hard. He had no chance of pretending that he wasn't turned on. He lowered his zipper to give his burgeoning erection some space.

"So what are you going to do about this?" Landry stuck a hand down his shorts.

"No touching, brat." Gage growled. "You have two minutes to get naked and be on the bed on all fours. One second longer, and you don't get to come tonight."

Landry's brain registered the threat as truth and he ran, pulling off his clothes as he went. Naked time with Gage was top of his list of the best ways to end the day.

Chapter Four

"My legs are aching. Can we find somewhere to sit a while?" Landry searched for a spot through the bustling crowds. "There sure are a lot of people here."

"This is one of those times when being vertically challenged is a disadvantage." Gage grabbed his arm. "I see a bench."

Landry went where Gage tugged him, weaving through the browsing shoppers at the market. "Oh thank goodness, and I am not short. I'm perfectly formed." He sank onto the bench, which was half-hidden behind a stall selling antiquarian books.

"Of course you're perfect, sweetheart. You want a soda? I could use a drink and maybe a snack. You can guard the bench."

"Iced coffee would be great and something sweet to nibble on."

"Why am I not surprised?" Gage walked off—his stride purposeful as if he knew where he was going. Landry slumped back on the bench. He lifted one foot at a time, rotating his ankles and wiggling his toes. He and Gage had walked the length of the flea market twice already, stopping at almost every stall to poke around. Landry had noted a few that he wanted to go back to. They hadn't bought anything yet, and he had spotted a lucky cat that he wanted to add to his collection. He sighed, content to sit with the sun warming his face. For once the forecast had been good, Gage had found a parking space nearby and the atmosphere at the market was friendly, if busy. Landry enjoyed the bustle. It wasn't often that Treasure Trove Antiques got crowded and it made a change to feel part of something bigger. He put his fatigue down to an exceptionally busy week.

Gage was only gone five minutes and he returned bearing a large take-out cup of iced coffee, a soda running with condensation, a hot dog with far too much onion spilling from the bun and a greasy paper bag, which he handed to Landry before joining him on the bench.

"I got you miniature donuts. They should still be hot. The guy fried them right there in front of me." He sat their drinks on the bench in between them.

"Oh my God, I love you so much." Landry delved in the bag, stuffing his face with greasy, sugar-coated goodness. "These are fantastic," he mumbled around his mouthful.

"When we finish this," Gage said, munching his dog, "how about we go back to the last couple stalls then call it a day?"

"Sure. If I walk much further my feet are going to fall off. We could go for a drive, if you like." Landry didn't want to slope off home if Gage wanted to spend more time out and about.

"Do I sound like a complete sap if I say I just want to go back to our place to be with you?"

"Yep, complete sap. Squishiest Dom ever." Landry hid a smile.

"But I didn't say what I wanted to do with you when we get back there."

Landry took a long swallow of his iced coffee. If he'd been wearing a collar he'd definitely have had to loosen it. "We could skip those last stalls…"

"Oh no, anticipation is the best part of a Dom/sub relationship and besides, if we don't buy anything today, you'll be bitching about it for the rest of the month."

Landry was about to deny it, but then thought better of it. "You know me too well," he muttered.

"I do, don't I? Now let's go find that weird looking cat you spotted for your collection and let's hope that this time there are no messages written inside it."

They took their garbage to the nearest recycling trash can then meandered down the street to look for the stall Landry had found earlier. "There it is, and my cat is still there," Landry said. "Do you think the stallholder likes to haggle? He looks older than God."

"Just because he has white hair and a long beard doesn't mean he's ancient," Gage said. "Though I hope he hasn't been on his feet all day."

They approached the stall where the old man was unwrapping a box of stock and laying it on the tables, which were arranged around him in a U shape.

"Hello again, young man. Have you come back for the cat I saw you taking an interest in earlier?"

"You remember me?" Landry asked.

"You two are a striking couple. Difficult to forget, and I can also spot someone who is genuinely interested in what I'm selling rather than just browsing."

"I have a collection of lucky cats at home," Landry said.

"Well, in that case, this one must belong with you." The old man handed over the red and black ceramic cat.

"How much is it?"

"It's a gift."

"Oh, that's so kind of you, but I couldn't possibly take it without paying." Landry cradled the ornament.

"Well, perhaps there's something else you might like?"

Landry scanned the eclectic range of antiques spread in front of him. "That wasn't here earlier." He pointed out a mirror, the glass tarnished and mottled. It had an ornate, gilded frame, carved from what he guessed was a single piece of wood and an equally ornate handle. It was filthy, but through the dirt Landry could make out winding leaves and stems. The mirror had a beveled edge and blackened metal clasps holding it in place. He could tell that it was a high-quality piece, even if it had had a hard life.

"I just put that out. You have a good eye."

Landry preened. He handed his cat to Gage then picked up the mirror to take a closer look. It was surprisingly heavy and much bigger than the usual dressing table size. When he turned it over, there were no markings on the wooden back. "I'd guess this is early 1900s. It has an art nouveau feel about it."

"It's yours for fifty dollars."

"Are you sure? That seems so little for such a beautiful piece."

"Fifty dollars is the price, and you must promise to give the cat a good home."

"I will," Landry said, handing over some bills. "It's already bringing me some luck, it seems. You're absolutely sure about this?"

"Young man, do I look senile?"

Gage snorted. "Honey, thank the man. He has other customers waiting."

"Oh, sorry, I didn't notice." There was a short line hovering behind Landry. "Thank you so much."

Gage steered Landry away from the stall. "Give me the mirror. You can carry the cat."

"Not macho enough for you?"

"Landry…"

Landry handed over the mirror, which Gage tucked under his arm. "Gimme my cat." Landry stroked it then gave it a kiss. "You're gonna be right at home with my feline family, don't you worry."

"You're certifiable. Let's go." Gage led the way back to his Jeep because Landry, whose sense of direction was flawed at the best of times, had no clue where it was in relation to their current location. "It amazes me that you can make it from the store to the coffee shop and back without getting lost," Gage said.

"I did turn out of the café door the wrong way one time. I had this super large, caramel latte with whipped cream and chocolate sprinkles. It distracted me. I'd walked all the way past St. Peters before I realized I was heading in the wrong direction. Are we nearly there yet? I think I have a blister."

"You sound like a five-year-old but yes, the car is across the street."

"Yay!" Landry's energy returned and he bounced over to the Jeep. He scrambled into his seat while Gage wrapped the mirror in a blanket then laid it on the back seat. He brushed some dust from his hands. "That thing's filthy," he complained as he climbed behind the wheel.

"It'll be beautiful once I've cleaned it." Landry fiddled with the radio dial until he found a station playing Lady Gaga. "I suspect it's worth a lot more than I paid for it. I feel a bit guilty about paying so little."

"Perhaps the guy picked it up for next to nothing himself. I'm sure he made a profit on it. Will you sell it in the store?" Gage pulled out into the trickle of traffic.

"I might fall in love with it, then I won't be able to part with it."

"Is that what happened with me?" Gage grinned.

"Nah, you fell for me first 'cause I'm too adorable to resist."

"You're blushing."

"Keep your eyes on the road, Detective."

After a quick stop for supplies, Landry trudged up the stairs to the apartment. He carried his lucky cat and a bag of groceries while Gage lugged two more bags and the mirror. By the time the shopping was stowed, and the cat installed with its new companions on a shelf, Landry was wilting.

"I don't know what's wrong with me," he moaned, collapsing onto the couch. "I'm shattered."

"You do seem a bit pale." Gage pressed the backs of his fingers to Landry's forehead. "I think you might be coming down with something. You feel like you have a temperature and it's not like you to be so tired."

"I hate being ill. This only came on this morning so maybe I just need a nap. You wore me out last might. Another few hours and I'll be good."

"Why don't you get into bed? I'll get the thermometer from the first aid kit and find some Tylenol. If you are sick, we can get a head start on getting you better and if not, painkillers won't do you any harm."

"I don't have time to be ill. I have a store to run."

"You have time to do what I say." Gage narrowed his eyes. "If you're sick, we'll manage."

"I have a feeling your bedside manner is gonna suck." Landry hauled himself upright. "Ooh, did I have vodka because the room is kinda spinning?" Gage scooped him off his feet then carried him to the bedroom.

"Do you feel sick?" Gage plopped him onto the bed.

"No, but there's some pressure in my ear. Feels peculiar." Landry smacked the side of his head.

"Stop that!" Gage pulled his hand away. "Sounds like you have an ear infection."

"I did go to the pool one evening last week when you were working late. I could have picked it up there I suppose."

"You mean you actually swam rather than ogle that hot lifeguard you fancy?"

"He wears such teeny shorts and…wait, what? You've never been to the pool with me so how did you know…?"

"He's dating one of Sancha's cousins. Sancha and Ana had coffee, Ana told her about Kelly and where he works. You'd told Sancha you liked to swim at the same pool…it didn't take much coaxing before your dreamy-eyed gazes came out. Kelly likes to tell Ana about his regulars, apparently. Especially the characters."

"I'm ill…I'm not responsible for my actions, though I quite like the idea of being a character."

"You weren't ill when you went to the pool. This is karma. We'll be discussing your behavior in more detail when you're better. A lot more detail."

Landry pouted. "I'm taken, not dead. You should see those cute blue budgie smugglers, then you'd understand and besides, he's obviously straight."

"Budgie smugglers?"

"Australian for Speedos, though whoever came up with that term has serious issues."

"Huh. I understand perfectly by the way, and he's bi. He told Ana that if he hadn't been head over heels for her, he might have asked you on a date. He calls you blondie board shorts by the way."

"He gave me a nickname? That's adorable!"

"You wanna dig that hole a bit deeper?"

"You know I love you best, honeybuns." Landry pursed his lips in hope of a conciliatory kiss.

"Call me that ever again, and I'll gag you for an entire weekend." The kiss that followed was firm but brief.

"How can you be so mean to a sick person?"

"Take your clothes off, Landry and don't get any ideas. I'll fetch you a hot drink and those meds. The only thing on your schedule for the rest of the day is sleep."

* * * *

Thirty minutes later, Gage stood in the bedroom door watching Landry sleep. He was snoring, his mouth was open and he was clutching the plush alligator Sancha had given him for his birthday. A warm glow spread through Gage's body. *Shit, I have it bad.* He pulled the door, leaving it open a crack so that he could hear if Landry called out then strolled to where his laptop was set up on the dining table. He'd intended to earn some credit with Sancha by catching up on some paperwork. Instead, he called her.

"Hey, partner."

"Hey yourself. Why are you calling me on your day off? What did you do? And stop rolling your eyes."

Gage glanced around the apartment, hunting for concealed cameras. "Landry's sick. I'm worried."

"Oh no! What's up with my best boy?"

"Hey! I thought I was your best boy."

"Sorry honey, Landry is way cuter than you."

"Traitor. Just remember who has your back out there in the big, bad world. Landry has all the symptoms of an ear infection. He's sleeping but he's flushed and has a slight temperature. Do you think I should take him to the ER?"

"I'm not a doctor, Gage."

"You have kids. They get sick all the time. I'm sure you mentioned Jonas having an ear infection one time."

"Damn, you have a good memory. Jonas was only two when he had that. Did Landry throw up?"

"No. He has a headache and fatigue. He got tired when we were out earlier today, much quicker than he would usually because you know he's a ball of energy. He also said he had some pressure in his ear."

"He probably got it at the pool mooning over Ana's Kelly. Definitely sounds like an infection. Unless his temperature gets dangerously high, he should recover in a few days. He might get sick, and his hearing may be affected but the doc won't prescribe antibiotics initially. It's one of those things that gets better on its own."

"Good to know."

"If you're worried you could ask one of the EMTs from the fire house to drop by."

"I don't want to overreact. It just came on so quickly and Landry is hardly ever ill. His mom told me he has a stronger constitution than his brothers even though he's half their size."

"Ah yes, the Viking twins. Yum."

"You're shameless."

Sancha cackled. "No, I have great taste."

"And a husband."

"Pietro is also hot but that doesn't mean I'm blind."

"Hmm, Landry said something similar earlier when we were discussing the lifeguard at the pool. I need to keep a closer eye on that boy."

"Gonna chain him to the bed, huh? You have nothing to worry about where Landry is concerned. That boy thinks the sun shines out of your every orifice, which makes me doubt his sanity, but it takes all sorts I suppose."

"You have such an interesting turn of phrase."

"You know it. How about tomorrow, will you be working or staying home to nurse Landry?"

"I'll let you know in the morning once I get a picture of how he is. I'm going to call Mr. Lao next and let him know he may need to cover the store. Petey's not been around long enough to manage on his own for a whole day."

"Okay, well let me know if I can do anything. I make a mean chicken soup."

"You've never made that for me."

"Your man-flu doesn't count as a genuine illness, Gage."

"You're a hard woman."

"And you're pathetic when you're not healthy. I have enough of that with my other half — another man who thinks a head cold is a harbinger of death. Now go minister to the sick, I'll talk to you tomorrow."

Gage smiled as he ended the call. Sancha always managed to make him feel better and on this occasion, less prone to panic. He called Mr. Lao next who promised to bring some Chinese herbs with him the next day to make Landry a special tea, after assuring Gage that it would be no problem if Landry needed to spend the day in bed. Petey was last on the list but Gage's call went to voicemail, so he left a message, guessing that Petey was tied up with Carson. *Literally, knowing Carson.* Content that he'd done all he could to ensure things went smoothly the next day, Gage settled down to work. He and Sancha were hunting down a money laundering ring—people who enabled the worst of the worst to get away with murder. It was a multi-million-dollar business and had far-reaching implications, none of which were good. The people involved protected their interests with intimidation and violence. Gage couldn't wait to bring them down.

He worked for an hour or so but a huge yawn that made his jaw crack signaled it was time for bed. He debated sleeping on the couch to give Landry some space but dismissed it in favor of keeping his spine intact. A pillow-top mattress was not something to be rejected out of hand. He undressed in the dark then slipped beneath the covers. Landry snuffled then shoved his ass back into Gage's groin, muttering beneath his breath. He quieted when Gage flung an arm over him, holding him close. *Still trying to get his own way even when he's unconscious.* Gage wouldn't have it any different, he much preferred knowing exactly where Landry was. Much less chance of him getting into trouble that way.

Chapter Five

The next morning, Landry made it to the table in time to have breakfast with Gage. He didn't have much appetite but spooned down some cereal accompanied by an extra-strong coffee.

"How are you feeling? Are you sure you're well enough to go into the store this morning?" Gage asked.

"Stop fussing!" Landry patted Gage's hand. "It's not that bad. Besides, I'm only catching every other word, my head's all woolly. Like a sheep."

Gage scowled. "I think you should go back to bed. You need to rest."

"What's wrong with my head?" Landry patted his hair. "I might feel like a sheep but I don't want to look like one."

"You are treading on very thin ice, young man, sick or not."

Landry looked up at Gage from beneath his lashes. "I promise I'll be fine. I'll sit in the store cupboard where it's dark and quiet, then if Petey needs me, I'm there, and Mr. Lao doesn't need to be on his feet all day. He's old, you know." He stood, bowl in hand.

"He's fitter than I am, and that's so not the point. You're sick. You should stay home."

"You're a fine one to talk. When have you ever taken a sick day? Unless you have a straitjacket handy, you're not going to win this one. I have a slight headache and my hearing is a bit dodgy. My temperature has gone down—you took it yourself. I'm fine to work, it's not like I'm flying a plane or doing brain surgery."

"Doesn't mean you shouldn't be on your best form. Pity we don't own a rectal thermometer." Landry gasped and covered his backside with his free hand. "Heard that well enough then?"

"I think *you* should go to work. Sancha will do much worse to you if you're late."

"Unfortunately, that's true." Gage scowled, and Landry knew he'd won but managed to prevent a victorious grin. "Fine. You can go to the store but only if you promise me that the moment you feel bad, or if the fever comes back, you'll come up here to bed."

"Pinky swear." Once he'd cleared up the breakfast things, Landry didn't quite skip down the stairs to the store. He didn't feel *that* well. Gage waited until he was installed in the store cupboard with a mug of Mr. Lao's ginger tea and his new mirror to clean, then left for work after giving Petey a stern lecture on making sure Landry didn't over-tire himself.

When Gage had gone, Petey stuck his head around the store cupboard door. "Your boyfriend is scary intimidating," Petey said. "He said my life expectancy might reduce if I let you overexert yourself, or at the very least he'd tell Carson to find out how much I enjoyed CBT."

"He's a little overprotective. Ignore him, he's a squishy teddy bear really."

"Could have fooled me. I'm not risking getting my bits squashed in a clamp or some other fiendish torture device, thank you very much. I haven't seen the contents of Carson's toy box yet and I'm not sure I want to. He told me he really enjoys predicament bondage and, though I'm kind of intrigued, the idea also gives me the willies."

Landry snorted. "You said willies!"

"What are you, three?"

"I was never properly socialized as a child. I had to grow up with two hulking older brothers, remember?"

"Your brothers are rather delicious." Petey smacked his lips together.

"Do not go there. Never go there. I have a vivid imagination and I really don't want my brothers featuring in it." Landry made retching noises.

"Don't do that! Gage will hear and think you're sick."

"He's in his car on his way to work, Petey."

"Like that would stop him. Do you need anything? Mr. Lao says he's going to stay until lunchtime and he's promised to show me all the rare books and explain why they're valuable." Petey peered over Landry's shoulder. He had his mirror laid on a cloth on the worktable they used for cleaning and restoration. "That's pretty, at least, I think it is under all that grime."

"I picked it up at the pop-up flea market Gage and I went to yesterday. I'm going to spend the morning giving it a clean."

"Okay, well shout if you want anything. I'll go out for coffee in an hour or so. Do you think you can wait that long?"

"Sure. I'm going to be tasting ginger for the rest of the day, anyway. Mr. L's tea is surprisingly good. Don't tell him, though, he'll be unbearable if he thinks I like something other than coffee."

"Carson asked me if I had any ginger root last night, but I don't think he wanted it to make tea with. I didn't have any and I think that might have been a good thing."

Landry wriggled in his seat, imagining the burn that accompanied a good figging. "It's bad, in a good way. Or do I mean good in a bad way? My brain isn't working properly today."

"No kidding. I need to get to work. You should have warned me about the stare-thing Mr. Lao has going on by the way. The cute old guy is kinda scary too." Petey blew a kiss in Landry's direction. "Have fun."

Landry rolled his shoulders. Cleaning antiques was delicate work, and he needed to concentrate, not easy considering his headache was growing. He shrugged. *Bed's boring without Gage in it.* Before his mind could start wandering into territory involving Gage, bed and the resulting possibilities, Landry grabbed a soft rag. His first job was to remove as much surface dirt as possible. Once that was done, he'd use damp Q-tips to give it another going over.

The mirror's carved frame was intricate, full of curls and grooves, as was the handle, which was an inch shy of a foot long. Landry worked systematically from top to bottom. At some point Petey delivered a latte, which Landry drank on autopilot, but it wasn't until lunchtime that he realized he'd been bent over the mirror for almost four hours without a break. The work was paying off—all over the frame the gilt was beginning to show through, his body however, was protesting.

He stood, stretched then groaned as his head, shoulders, back and hips all joined forces to protest their mistreatment. Petey stuck his head around the door.

"Oh, you look like crap!"

"Thanks, Petey—just the motivational comment I need from my best friend."

"Well you do, and I don't want Gage to shoot me—he has a big gun. You need to go to bed."

"No."

"Yes!"

"Could you cut the decibels?" Landry knuckled his temples.

"If you don't go upstairs to your apartment, I'm gonna start singing some Kylie."

"You're tone deaf. When you sing, animals start evacuating like there's a volcanic eruption or tsunami on the way."

"Exactly."

"Fine. I'll go make myself a sandwich then work upstairs for a while." Tucking the mirror under his arm, Landry levered himself upright. "I think I did that too quickly… Why is everything moving?"

"The ear infection is probably affecting your balance, you idiot."

"No kidding…" Landry made a grab for the edge of his table, missed and went to his knees, knocking his face on the corner of the table as he went. "Oh, ow!" He managed to save the mirror before it hit the ground, but the rear panel dislodged. He shuffled back on his ass so that he could lean against the wall and laid the mirror across his thighs. He rubbed at his face. "That hurt.

Landry versus the table is not a good idea. At least it was me that got damaged and not my mirror."

"Has anyone ever told you that your priorities are completely wrong?" Petey scowled. "Gage is going to do bad things to me when he sees your face."

"Did you just whimper? Help me up, and I'll go hide upstairs. By the time Gage gets home the redness will have gone, and you'll have Carson to protect you. I don't think it's bad enough to bruise anyway."

"Sounds like a terrible plan." Holding out a hand, Petey waited while Landry laid the mirror on the floor before heaving himself to his feet. This time, Landry waited a while before attempting to move. Petey bent down to pick up the mirror. "The wooden retaining panel has slipped a bit. Doesn't look like any of the catches have snapped, though."

"Oh, that's good. I was going to take the back off anyway, so that I could clean underneath. I don't know what I would have done if the glass had broken. Apart from Lord knows how many years' bad luck, I'd never have found a replacement."

"You're not going to put a new piece in?" Petey ran a finger down the mottled glass.

"No, I like the aged look. And besides, it's more valuable with the original in there."

After reassuring Petey that he could make the trip unaided, Landry kept close to the wall as he made his way out of the storage room and around the back of the store to the door that led to the hallway. If he got giddy again, he wanted something solid to lean on. As a teenager he'd been on a school trip to Mount Rainier. The stairs seemed steeper and more of a challenge than the mountain ever had. By the time he reached the landing outside his apartment door, Landry was panting and giving thanks that he'd moved one floor down from the attic. "Going back to bed might not be such a bad idea after all," he muttered. "You're never too old to nap."

Leaving the mirror on the dining table, he grabbed a bottle of apple juice from the fridge before making his way to the bedroom. His head was pounding, and his vision dark around the edges. He managed to kick off his shoes and drink the juice before collapsing onto the bed with a moan. Sleep claimed him before his first sheep bounced over the stile.

When he came to, Landry had no idea how long he'd been asleep. The room was dark, and the curtains drawn, something he couldn't remember doing. The mattress shifted, and he realized he wasn't alone. "Gage?"

"You'd better hope so. Before you ask, yes, Petey is still alive, though it was a close thing. How are you feeling?" Gage laid cool fingers on Landry's forehead.

Landry lay still and thought about it. "Actually, I feel okay."

"You sound surprised."

"Well... I needed a nap, and my head was hurting when I went to sleep. I kept getting dizzy but now the headache has gone, and I can move without feeling like I need to throw up." He struggled into a sitting position. "What time is it?"

"Nearly eight. I got home a half-hour ago."

"Wow, I've been asleep over six hours."

"Which you wouldn't have needed if you'd done what I suggested this morning and stayed home to rest."

"Maybe?"

"No doubt about it." Gage stroked Landry's hair. "Perhaps we need to formalize the necessity that you be obedient in a contract."

"Or I could admit you were right and promise to listen in future?"

"Hmm. Sounds like deflection to me."

"You can spank me when I'm feeling better."

"Oh, I can, can I?"

"Uh huh, if you want to of course...I mean, that's up to you, Sir." Landry gulped. "I'm so thirsty, could I have some ginger tea?"

"More deflection."

"I slept in my clothes. I should take a shower too."

"You get a pass today and possibly tomorrow, but that's it. By the end of the week your ass will be on fire and your dick will be in a cage." Gage stomped off in the direction of the kitchen.

Landry flopped back on the bed. "Phew. Lucky escape."

"I heard that!"

"Do you have super-powered ears?"

"All the better to hear you with." There was a certain amount of intriguing menace in Gage's tone.

"I need to invest in a red cloak," Landry muttered. "That man definitely has wolfish tendencies."

"Still listening!"

"Damn it!" Landry stripped off his clothes then sprinted to the bathroom. At least with the shower running he could talk to himself in peace.

Half an hour later, Landry was in the middle of inhaling a particularly good bowl of chili. "This is so yum!"

"Don't speak with your mouth full." Gage grinned despite the admonishment.

Landry waved his now empty fork around. "You love it when I compliment your cooking."

"I like to see you enjoying it. The compliments aren't needed."

"Well, you need to accept them with grace because if you keep this up, there'll be more. It really is good, Gage. Are there any seconds? I didn't have any lunch." Landry hid his smile as Gage pretended to be grumpy while he went to fetch more food.

"Here you go. I made a big batch. We can freeze the rest."

"You're not having any more?"

"I'm full. I'll watch you stuff yourself."

"That sounds naughty."

"Eat, Landry!"

"I could get used to you waiting on me," Landry said, finally pushing his empty bowl away.

"You can dream. If you weren't ill, you'd be tied to your chair by now. Naked, of course."

"Oh, of course." Landry rolled his eyes. "And what would you be doing?"

"I'd be clamping those pretty nipples then running a pinwheel up and down your cock."

The heat built in Landry's cheeks and it wasn't the fever returning. Being ill apparently had no effect on his ability to achieve an erection. He shuffled in his seat, scowling at Gage's knowing grin.

"Now see what you did!" Landry waved at his lap.

"There does seem to be some swelling," Gage observed, peering over the edge of the table. "Is that usually a side effect of an ear infection?"

"It's a side effect of a Gage obsession," Landry muttered.

"Then we should treat it." Gage rose, stalked over to Landry's chair then lifted it, Landry still on it, until it faced away from the table. He sank to his knees between Landry's legs, yanked down his zipper and frowned. "Hmm, looks serious." Landry shifted so that Gage could yank pants and underwear down to Landry's ankles. "Kick them off then spread your legs."

Landry kicked frantically until the annoying garments flew in various directions leaving him clad only in socks and T-shirt. He parted his knees as wide as he could, and his rigid dick bounced until Gage ducked his head, taking Landry's erection into his mouth.

"Holy fuck!" Landry's voice rose between the first and second words. In a timescale he wasn't proud of, approximately twenty seconds, Landry came. He rose an inch or so off the seat, until Gage shoved him down again, and let out a wail that was going to give Petey nightmares if he didn't have his headphones on. Panting, Landry squirmed. Gage was still sucking, and it was too much, Landry's dick was too sensitive. Gage gave the tip of Landry's cock a final lick.

"Feeling better? The swelling seems to have gone down." He got to his feet and pulled Landry into his arms.

"I'm a bit dizzy and my knees are shaking."

"That doesn't sound good." Gage hoisted him up, both hands beneath his bare ass. "I'm gonna put you back to bed."

"Wait! I wanted to show you what I've done to my mirror."

"Okay. Five minutes." Gage didn't put Landry down.

"Uh, Gage?"

"What?"

"It's kind of hard for me to show you like this."

"Oh...sorry. Got a bit distracted by the feel of your...never mind." He put Landry on his feet. The mirror was still where Landry had left it, on the edge of the table. He reached for it but knocked it and the mirror tilted, swaying precariously. As it fell, Gage grabbed it. "Wow, good reflexes!"

"I think the back panel might be broken." Gage turned the mirror over then placed it on the table again.

"I should put my pants on."

"No."

"No?"

"You don't need pants."

Grumbling under his breath, Landry sat his ass down. "It dislodged a bit earlier when I almost dropped it in the store. I lost my balance. It's even looser now, but I was going to take it off this evening anyway, to clean the catches and take the glass out." Four metal clasps held the wooden backing in place, though three were now doing the job. Landry slid the panel free. "There's something here!"

"What is it?" Gage leaned over his shoulder.

"A folded piece of paper—looks old." Landry fumbled to get it out. He unfolded it, then smoothed it onto the dining table. He stared at it, trying to work out what it portrayed.

"It looks like a map," Gage said, leaning to take a closer look. "I think all the squiggles are contour lines."

"You could be right!" Landry traced one of the lines with the tip of his finger. "In which case, this is steep terrain. Some of these other marks look like they could be topographical symbols. There's a very faint cross here, could be a church." He fought back a yawn.

"And there will be plenty of time to have a closer look tomorrow," Gage said.

Landry was torn between wanting to keep looking at his new treasure map and the draw of a comfortable bed. "It's bedtime." Gage's expression suggested that it wasn't the time to start an argument.

"Okay."

"You must be feeling bad," Gage said. "I was expecting much more of an argument. How did you get that red mark on your cheek, by the way?"

"I caught my face in the store when I lost my balance earlier today. It's nothing."

"Did you think I wouldn't notice? It's going to bruise." Gage touched Landry's face.

"I got a bit dizzy, that's all."

Gage scooped Landry off his chair and into his arms. "All the more reason to put you to bed."

Landry flailed then relaxed into Gage's hold. He snuggled against Gage's chest. "Promise we can spend time on the map tomorrow?"

"No promises until I know how you're feeling. You might need a day in bed."

"No!" Landry wailed. "What if it's a treasure map? I need to find out if X marks the spot."

"You have an overactive imagination." Gage gave Landry's bare ass a pat then dropped him onto the bed.

"And that is not a bad thing. You wouldn't like me nearly so much if I didn't."

"What makes you think I like you?" Gage stripped off his clothes then stood naked at the foot of the bed, hands on hips.

Landry licked his lips. "Well, there's one clue, right there." He waggled his finger in the direction of Gage's dick. "You love me. I am very lovable and impossible to resist. What are you going to do about that hard pointy thing?"

"You're sick. Take the rest of your clothes off. You need rest."

"I'm still capable of lying here with my mouth open," Landry said. "An ear infection doesn't affect my jaw muscles, or my tongue…" He yelped as Gage clambered onto the bed then crawled over him. He set about removing Landry's remaining clothing as fast as possible until they were both equally bare. Landry grinned up at him, delighted at the reaction he had inspired.

"So maybe I do love you." Gage prodded at Landry's lips with the end of his cock. "Open up and take your medicine."

"Yes, Doctor…" Any more words were cut off. Gage grabbed the headboard and bounced in place while Landry could only lie there and take it. There was no opportunity for licking or sucking because not gagging took all Landry's concentration. He reached for Gage's ass and managed to gain some purchase, digging his fingers into flexing muscle.

"Fuck, fuck…" Gage came in a series of hot spurts down Landry's throat, his face contorted into a grin grimace combination. He pulled clear but remained where he was while he took a few heaving breaths. Landry ran his tongue over his lips then let go of Gage's backside.

"I may have given you bruises," he said happily. Gage frowned and rubbed at his rear. "I needed something to hang onto."

"Brat." Gage shuffled to one side of the bed. "Lift your butt so I can sort the covers." A lot of wiggling followed until they both made it beneath the comforter and Landry found his happy place spooned into Gage's groin. "How are your ears?"

"Ringing. I'm thinking of taking up campanology."

"Go to sleep, Landry."

"Yes, Sir." Landry closed his eyes. The sooner sleep came the sooner the treasure hunt could begin.

Chapter Six

"Nooo!" Landry wailed as the bell above the shop door rang again and a crowd of soggy people herded inside. "Why does it have to be so busy today?"

"Why? Do you have somewhere better to be?" Petey asked. "You've been acting like you have ants in your pants all day. Ooh, did Gage stuff something interesting up your... Good afternoon, madam, is there something I can help you with?"

Landry withheld a snort as he watched Petey sweet talk his latest customers. Sadly, Gage hadn't done anything nefarious that morning. They'd both overslept, and there had been no time for anything except showers and emergency coffee. Landry felt much better, with no headache or giddiness, but his hearing was still a bit muffled. Over the phone, he'd assured Mr. Lao that he was more than capable of handling the store for the day. Now, though, he was regretting his bravado. Not because he'd had a relapse but because they'd been so busy he hadn't had a chance to examine his map. Rainy days at Treasure Trove seemed to go one of two ways. Either the weather kept everyone hunkered down at home and the store remained deserted or the entire antique-buying population of Seattle decided enough was enough and braved the downpour for a spot of retail therapy. Today, the world and his wife seemed to fancy perusing old furniture while sheltering from the persistent precipitation. Sales had been great and that meant good commission for Landry as well as plenty of room for new stock, but all Landry could think about was the map. He wrapped a set of champagne flutes on autopilot, nodding to the customer while not really following what they were saying. When they eventually left and Petey finished with the lady he was dealing with, Landry heaved a sigh of relief. The store was finally empty.

"What's up with you?" Petey asked. "You've been acting strange all day. Should you go and rest? If your head is hurting, you need to say so because I value my dangly bits. Carson likes them, and I like Carson liking them."

"Way too much information there, Petey! I'm fine. Not caffeinated enough... But am I ever?"

Petey gaped. "I have no idea how to respond to that."

"If you go get drinks, I'll tell you a secret," Landry said. "I'll pay."

"What kind of secret? Is it worth my while because I know all about your illicit desire to stick your tongue up Gage's..."

"This is another secret... A better one, and you shouldn't talk about the other thing out loud because I'm ninety-nine percent sure Gage has installed listening devices all over the store."

Pete's eyes widened and he scanned the shelves. "He would so do that."

"Even more reason for you to fetch me coffee."

"Fine but I want extra gold stars for going out in the rain to satisfy your addiction."

"And you're not going to enjoy the hot chocolate with whipped cream and sprinkles I know you're going to get for you?"

"Well, it's a hot chocolate kind of day, though we should also have an open fire and marshmallows to toast. Oh! I can get marshmallows in my chocolate... Give me the money."

Landry handed over some cash. "Don't forget my vanilla shot."

"As if." Petey skipped down the aisle and out of the door without stopping to put on a jacket or take an umbrella.

"He's gonna get wet," Landry muttered. While Petey was gone Landry cleared some space on the cash desk, pulled up two stools then fetched the map from the storeroom where he had hidden it behind a particularly ugly bronze of a rearing horse. A horse that in his opinion looked more like a donkey.

He smoothed out the brittle paper then fetched a battered angle poise lamp for better light. The lines and markings on the paper were faded from age and quite hard to see. The light was a distinct improvement but the more he stared at the map the less sense it seemed to make. He raked his fingers through his hair before trying to ease the crick in his neck. His joints gave a resounding crack just as Petey returned. The bell above the door jangled, and Petey came inside ass first, balancing two extra-tall cups. He shook his head like a dog, sending droplets flying.

"Hey! Stop getting the antiques wet," Landry shouted.

"It's not just raining cats and dogs out there, there's an entire petting zoo falling out of the sky."

Landry thought about that for a moment then grinned. He grabbed his coffee from Petey. "Wouldn't it be great if it did rain small furry things? We could have a pets' corner in the store to keep the kids entertained."

"You mean to keep you entertained." Petey shivered. "I'm soaked through. You mind if I run upstairs to change my T-shirt and dry my hair a bit? I'll be five minutes."

"You think maybe you should have worn a coat? Go ahead. You do look like a drowned rat. Oh, we should have a movie night when Gage is working late. We could watch *Ratatouille*."

"You want to watch a cartoon rat when we could be ogling Jason Momoa?"

"Good point, but the rat is cute too."

"Hey, I'm not judging but I'm not into the furries. If you and Gage want to dress up in fuzzy costumes, you go for it." Petey ran for the stairs before Landry could deliver the smack he was aiming at his backside.

He's getting to be as cheeky as I am. I'm gonna have to up my game.

While he was waiting for Petey to return, Landry grabbed a mop from the back hall then ran it over the main aisle. He didn't want anyone face planting because Petey had dripped everywhere. He glanced outside to confirm there was no chance of the downpour letting up anytime soon—the weather seemed set to last for hours. He turned on another lamp near the rare books to cheer up the gloom. Mop in hand he scanned the books, running his fingers over embossed spines, the gold reminding him of his mirror. One of the larger books caught his attention, and he pulled it from the shelf.

"*The Art of Cartography*—that could be useful." He took the book with him, stored the mop then returned to the cash desk just as Petey reappeared.

"I want hot chocolate and secrets. You'd better not have snaffled my drink."

"I was cleaning up after your soggy ass." Landry slipped his book onto the shelf under the cash desk before grabbing his coffee.

"What's that?" Petey swung his cup-holding hand precariously close to the map.

"Careful!" Landry steered his arm away. "That's my secret. I found the map hidden in the back of my mirror."

"Wow! That's so exciting. Is it a treasure map? It must be if it was hidden, mustn't it?"

"I hope so, but so far I haven't had a chance to decipher it. Gage reckons all the squiggles are contour lines, and I think he might be right. There are some symbols and what I think are letters, but the ink is faded."

"I was in the orienteering team during high school, I know all about map symbols and geography was always my best subject."

"Then you can be chief treasure-hunting assistant. Mr. Lao keeps a magnifying glass in the store cupboard, wanna fetch it?"

"Sure. You know, if it is a treasure map, there could be invisible ink, or a code or something." Petey kept talking while he fetched the magnifying glass.

"I'd prefer it to be something real simple, like a big red X and a detailed description of the location," Landry said.

"That's never the way it happens on TV or in books. Did you not read the *Da Vinci Code*?"

"If it's that complicated the two of us don't stand a chance."

"Isn't it in the best friend rulebook that you don't insult me?" Petey's indignation made Landry laugh.

"The rulebook I have has it top of the list."

"Color me not surprised." Petey squinted through the magnifying glass at the map. "I wonder if there's some clever gizmo on the Internet, which can identify where contour lines are in the world."

"Not that I've been able to find," Landry said. "It was the first thing I thought of. We should invent that, or at least patent the idea or something then one of those big tech companies can buy it from us for millions of dollars."

"If we're going to do that, we won't need to go treasure hunting."

"This is more exciting. Keep your fingers crossed we don't get any more customers. I can't believe how much stuff we've sold today. Enough to reach our target for the week."

"We should be grateful," Petey said, "not looking to put off prospective buyers."

"There's a rare books store I follow on Twitter called Sotheran's. It's kind of ancient, and their social media guy posts the funniest stuff about how they don't want to sell the books. They have an owl, and a ghost and people send him tinned tuna."

"Where's that then, New York?"

"London. Don't think I'll be getting to visit any time soon."

"Me either," Petey said. "But wouldn't that be the most amazing trip? We'd have so much fun. Carson was telling me about this firefighter exchange program. He has a buddy in the UK called Beau. It was fate they got matched up because this guy is as kinky as Carson and he's a member of this amazing club called The Underground. If we ever get over there, we'll have to go. That reminds me, Carson was talking about us having an outing to Scorch pretty soon."

"That sounds great. The last time Gage and I went we were both so tired it was all we could do to sit in the corner and cuddle. Not exactly hard-core."

Petey chuckled. "No one judges at Scorch. Map first, kink later. If we can't work any of this out, you'll have to get Gage to help, the man has skills."

"He sure does." Landry's mind drifted a little.

"Earth to Landry, earth to Landry, come in, please. I know where your head just went and it had nothing to do with topographical symbols, did it?"

"It's your fault, mentioning Gage's skills. What did you expect?"

"I was talking about his detecting skills. Jesus, you have a one-track mind."

"And you don't? It's a very nice track."

"So not the point. Do you want to look at the map or not?"

After some elbowing and jostling they both got into a position where they could see, sharing the magnifying glass between them.

"If these are contour lines, and I think they probably are, this could be a canyon or gorge," Petey said. "At the very least, a valley with very steep sides. The line at the bottom could be water, or a path. Without color there's no way of knowing."

"If it is a canyon, it looks like there's a church at one end. What's that symbol?" Landry pointed out a mark that resembled a line drawing of a picnic table with a dot underneath it.

"I think it might be a mine entrance but I'm not absolutely sure. Better check that online."

Landry heaved his book from under the counter. "I have an actual book. It's all about cartography. We had it in stock."

"Wow. Old school."

"I read."

"Yeah, on your e-reader. Or manga comics."

"Don't get me started on the joys of yaoi. I'll get distracted, and we'll get nowhere."

Landry found a section of the book that listed map symbols from various decades. They hadn't changed a great deal. "You're right. It's a mine entrance." Petey preened. "So we have a church at the end of a valley or canyon, a mine entrance in the canyon and a possible stream. It's not much to go on, there must be hundreds of mines in the US and thousands of churches. We can probably rule out the flat states because of the terrain, but that doesn't narrow it down much at all." Landry huffed his frustration.

"Well, if somebody hid something they didn't want found, interpreting this map isn't going to be easy," Petey said. "If there are clues, they might only mean something to the person who made the map."

"That's so depressing. It could take us months to find a possible match just by looking at maps."

"It would be good if we had a way of dating it, too." Landry yawned. "I'm still a bit wiped out from this ear infection. It's hard to concentrate when there's this muffled ringing in my ears."

"You came back to work too soon."

"It was that or go stir-crazy in the apartment. I'm not designed to spend lots of time on my own. My mind tends to misbehave and come up with the kind of plans that get me into trouble."

"You definitely shouldn't be allowed out unsupervised, that's for sure."

"You sound like Gage."

"I wouldn't normally side with him over you, but he knows you. You have a habit of attracting trouble and don't give me that big-eyed innocent look. I know you even better than he does."

"I feel persecuted," Landry muttered. "But thinking about the Dommy one, which I do a lot, how would he approach this?"

"Carson would just lecture me about how paper is an incendiary material. He's obsessed with fire safety."

"And then you could start discussing how effective his hose is," Landry cackled. "Oh no, is that a customer?" The bell over the shop door rang.

"It's Gage. You think he knew we were talking about him?"

"We were actually talking about Carson's hose," Landry said, giggling.

"Do I want to know?" Gage approached the cash desk, his hair glistening with raindrops and the shoulders of his jacket darkened by water. He leaned in for a kiss. "No! Don't get water on my map." Landry scampered around the cash desk to claim his kiss in safety.

"Have you two been playing detective?" Gage asked once they'd separated.

"We are not playing," Landry protested. "This is serious stuff."

"Then what does Carson's firehose have to do with it?"

"Nothing. Petey is easily distracted."

"Hey!" Petey stuck his tongue out. "You're the one that got off track. Perhaps you can help us, Gage? We think we might be being a bit obvious. How would you investigate the map?"

"We've identified the symbols, but other than that we're not getting very far, and they don't help us narrow down location much." Landry tugged Gage over to have a look. "Are you staying or do you have to go back to work?"

"I'm on a flying visit to check if it's okay for Sancha to come for dinner tonight. Her in-laws have the kids, and Pietro is having a boys' night out."

"Of course," Landry said. "She's welcome any time, you know that."

"Sure but I thought you might need me to go to the store for extra supplies. I wasn't sure what you had planned for tonight's dinner."

"Good point. How about grilled chicken, stuffed baked potatoes and a side salad? I have everything I need for that, but you could pick up something for dessert and maybe a bottle of wine. Sancha doesn't get a night off very often, I'm sure she'd like a drink or two."

"Will do. Let me take a look at this thing. Have you thought about the paper the map is on rather than just looking at the drawing?" Gage held the map up beneath the angle poise lamp. "Looks like there's a watermark of some kind, perhaps that will give you a clue."

"Unbelievable," Landry muttered. "You're here three minutes and find something we didn't even consider. So not fair."

Gage rolled his eyes. "You've either got it or you haven't." He caught Landry's glare and backed away. "I'll be going back to detecting now." He jogged down the aisle then out into the rain.

"You do that, or you'll be the one needing a safe word later," Landry shouted after him. He huffed. "You can stop laughing too, Petey."

"You guys are too funny."

"Do you and Carson want to come to dinner? Not that you deserve it."

"Oh that would be fun, I love Sancha. I'll text Carson."

"I'd better up the dessert order. If Gage gets anything involving chocolate, we won't get a look in with Sancha at the table." He sent Gage a text while Petey got in touch with Carson. "If Carson can't make it, it's no problem having left over dessert." Landry held the map up to the light. "I can't believe I didn't think of this. The watermark has a name and a date. Bellingham, 1946." He did a quick sketch of the mark. It was circular, the words written in uppercase inside two outer rings. In the center circle was a line drawing of a framed portrait. "This gives us something to research. The map could be a red herring."

"It's a starting point. We can get everyone to help over dinner. Ooh, customers!" Several bedraggled people came in. "You put that away, and I'll go help."

Landry put the map back in its hiding place, resigned to a wait before he could carry on researching. He turned to thinking about dinner—spontaneous plans with friends were his favorite. A mystery to solve would make the gathering even more fun.

Chapter Seven

Gage didn't look at his messages until he got back to work and was sat across the desk from Sancha. "Landry says to get extra dessert because Carson and Petey may be joining us for dinner."

"Cool. Petey is darling, and Carson is the best kind of eye candy. He could give me the kiss of life any day."

Gage shook his head. "The whole gay Dom thing not putting you off?"

"I don't discriminate. Hot is hot."

"Good Lord."

"What dessert are we getting?"

"You're worse than Landry. I'm less important to him than peach pie, did you know that?"

"He has a point, but chocolate silk would beat you *and* peach. They have them at that fancy patisserie about three blocks from Treasure Trove."

"Fine. We'll drive by later. We still have a few hours' work to do, though, so stop drooling."

Sancha scowled. "Dessert choices are more stimulating than paperwork, and you know how I feel about chocolate."

"I hope Pietro knows he has a rival for your affections and tell me about it." Gage eyed the foot-high pile of paper in his in-tray. "I thought this was supposed to be a paperless office now."

"Yeah, and that's a purple-spotted hippo I see flying past the window."

Sancha's desk phone rang, so Gage begun rifling through folders while she took the call. When she slammed the phone down, Gage gave her a curious look. "What's up?"

"I may have to start believing in those purple hippos. A contact of mine just gave me some very interesting information. You know when Petey was attacked, he was on his way to deliver a parcel?"

"Yes, to the building next to Scorch. An accountant's office."

"So we were led to believe, and there is an accountancy business registered to that address, but turns out it's a cover."

"Are you going to tell me what for, or am I going to have to guess?" Gage folded his arms and scowled.

"I should make you guess, but I'm too excited. There was an accountant based there until two years ago. They relocated to Denver and since then the place has housed a firm that imports and exports precious gems. A diamond merchant, though they deal in all kinds of stones. The fact that they are hiding their presence puts my hackles up." Sancha drummed her fingers on the desk. "It could be innocent because I doubt they want to broadcast their presence for security reasons, but still…"

"We've been looking into the obvious ways of hiding money in this laundering case," Gage mused. "Nowadays, it's mostly done electronically, via Internet businesses and so on. I thought criminals had moved away from precious metals and stones, but maybe I was wrong." He grabbed a pen and tapped it on his notepad. "When you think about it, what better way to keep us off track than by going back to an old trick? It's possible it could be a legitimate business concerned about their security but why keep old signage up?"

"Call me cynical, but I think the place stinks like a ten-day old haddock."

"I'm not going to ask how you know how that smells but I'm inclined to agree. I guess that means Petey could be more than the victim of a simple mugging. He could be a witness to a much more significant crime."

"Did he see anything?" Sancha sounded worried. "He couldn't identify his attackers or give a description."

"He could only say there were two of them, he saw their feet, but they won't know that. They may well think they killed him. If they find out he's alive then track him down, he could be in danger."

Sancha's eyes grew wider. She opened her mouth to speak but before she could utter a word Gage shoved his chair back and stood. "Fuck, that means Landry is in danger too." He grabbed his cell and stabbed at the menu to get Treasure Trove's number. "Landry, it's Gage. Are you and Petey alone in the store?"

"What's going on, Gage? You sound funny."

"Please answer the question."

"No, we're not alone. There are a bunch of customers in here, which I need to be helping. Carson just got back from his shift and he's lurking in a corner somewhere."

"Put Carson on the line."

"Why?"

"Not now, Landry. I need to talk to Carson."

"Fine."

Gage listened to Landry's muffled mutterings as he made his way to Carson. Several different voices were apparent in the background.

"Carson, I've got Gage on the phone and for some reason he won't tell me why he needs to talk to you. It'd better be to discuss dessert options, or I'm going to be very unhappy."

Gage gripped the back of his chair, holding back a snarl of impatience.

"Gage?"

"Carson, thank the Lord. Can you move somewhere out of Landry's earshot?"

"Sure, I'll go stand outside in the porch. Can't go much further because there's still a deluge going on out there. What's going on?"

Gage gave Carson a very brief summary of the situation and the possible danger. "Don't leave the two of them alone in the store, okay? Sancha and I will be there when we can but we have a new lead to run down. Keep your eye on the customers. Look out for anyone that doesn't fit in."

"Sure. I can hang out here. There's quite a crowd in the store but none of them look suspicious to me. They're all either buying weird stuff or asking questions that I don't understand. What the hell is rococo?"

"How the fuck should I know? I could be being paranoid, but if Petey did see something, even if he's not aware of it, that could make him a loose end in a very nasty case. There's a lot of money and powerful people involved in this, and we're getting closer. They'll be digging holes to hide in as fast as they can."

"You want me to say anything to Landry or Petey? They're gonna wonder why I'm not going to the apartment to change and get a shower."

"What do you think?"

Carson chuckled. "Landry's gonna smack your behind when he finds out you're keeping something from him."

"We can tell them later when we're together, but I don't want either of them worrying until they have to."

"Okay, I get it, but if things get heated, I'm blaming everything on you."

Gage snorted. "Go pretend to be doing a fire safety check or something. I'll see you later." He disconnected the call. "Carson is going to stay with the boys. I'd rather be there myself but I think we should go pay a visit to our gem dealer."

Sancha was already shrugging on her coat. "Let's go. Maybe I can pick out a diamond for my next birthday gift."

"Let's hope not. Pietro and I are friends and I'd quite like for us to stay that way."

"Not even a teeny weeny one?"

"Be grateful for the bottle of perfume you know he's going to get you."

"I'll bet Landry would like a diamond."

"He also likes alligators. He's not getting a real one of those either."

Sancha parked her car a block away from Scorch, not wanting to alert anyone to their presence. It was already getting dark, and the sidewalks were crowded with commuters hurrying toward the subway and the bus depot. Gage led the way, his intimidating presence helping to part the crowds until they turned off the main drag to a quieter side street. A garbage crew was at work, making Gage think how lucky Petey had been not to be scooped up by the trash compactor.

"Makes me shudder thinking about it," Sancha said, her mind apparently in the same place. "That was a pretty ruthless thing to do."

"They got what they wanted. I'd love to know what was in that package that was worth risking a murder charge."

Gage was very familiar with the street leading to Scorch, a route he'd followed many times, though he hadn't taken any notice of the nondescript premises on either side of the club. As they approached he was more observant than usual. The buildings on the block weren't modern. They were sturdy, red brick constructions with narrow windows and recessed doors. Scorch had once been four separate premises before being knocked through to make a much larger space. To the far side, the four stories housed an art collective, rainbow flags in every window. The fake accountancy firm had bars on every window and a sturdy door.

"A shitload of security for a bunch of number jockeys," Sancha observed.

"Sure is. Can't believe I haven't noticed it before, I'm down here often enough."

"But you're here at night, so you'd expect it to be all locked up, wouldn't you?"

"I guess, and I'm always with Landry so my attention is elsewhere." Gage contemplated the building. "How do you want to do this?"

"Straightforward knock on the door," Sancha said. "We're just making some inquiries, on official police business, so no need to bust anything down yet."

"There's a light on in one corner of the top floor," Gage observed. He went over to the door. There was no bell or knocker, so he hammered on it with his fist, the sound surprisingly loud in the quiet street. He took a step back and made sure he had easy access to his gun. Sancha stood a few paces away so they didn't present an easy target. Gage was about to knock again when he heard scuffling behind the door then the sound of chains rattling and locks disengaging. It swung open to reveal a short, pasty-skinned man with receding hair and a straggly moustache.

"Are you the proprietor of this business?" Gage asked, displaying his warrant card. Sancha mirrored his actions.

The man grinned. "Nah. I'm the custodian, fixing a leak in the bathroom. There's nobody else here. They've all gone."

"Gone as in gone for the day or gone for good?" Sancha asked.

"Above my pay grade. I just fix what I'm told to fix. You wanna come in and take a look around? I'm Cyril, Cyril Kazlo."

"Sure, that'd be great." Sancha gave him a reassuring smile. Gage kept his expression blank. When he and Sancha played good cop, bad cop, he was inevitably mister obnoxious. Cyril led the way inside to a boarded hallway, with peeling paint and a single, flickering strip light.

"Down here is just this storage closet for cleaning materials that kind of thing," he said, shoving open the single door.

Gage took a quick look inside, but it seemed to be as Cyril had described. Metal racking held bulk packs of toilet rolls, cleaning fluids, stationery — all the things an active business might get through regularly. He grunted. "Let's take a look upstairs."

"Sure. Next floor is office space then above that are the meeting rooms. Top floor is a staff break room, restrooms that type of thing. It's a narrow building, not much here."

Gage brought up the rear as the three of them formed a procession up the stairs. "And there's nobody here?"

"I haven't been into the office," Cyril said. "But I guess I would have heard if anyone was still around."

The door from the stairwell to the office wasn't locked. Gage pushed it open, searched for a light switch then turned it on. More flickering strip lights illuminated the space, and it was immediately obvious that it had been vacated in a hurry. There were no computers on any of the four desks, papers were scattered around the room and someone had been frantically shredding, leaving the machine overflowing.

"Well, I'll be..." Cyril shook his head. "The landlord is not going to like this."

"The company doesn't, didn't, own the building then?" Sancha asked.

"No, it's owned by a property company downtown. They have several buildings in Seattle and they use the services group I work for to do the maintenance, cleaning, that kind of thing. We cover about ten of their buildings across the city. The call for the repair I'm here to do was logged two days ago but this was the first chance I had to get over here. It's been stupid busy, ya know how it is."

"Cyril, why don't you show me the rest of the building while my partner here has look around the office?" Sancha suggested.

"Sure thing, lady. Ain't much more to see, though."

Once Sancha and Cyril had left, Gage donned a pair of latex gloves and began a systematic search for anything interesting. The paperwork would have to be gathered up to be examined in more detail, but he wanted to see if there were any obvious clues to what had been going on. On the floor next to the shredder he found some invoices that referred to carats and on a pin board on the wall, there was a tourist brochure about Amsterdam that sparked his interest. He pulled open desk drawers, feeling underneath them, scanned shelves and rummaged through bins but nothing else caught his attention. He put a call in for a crew to come and do a forensic search and gather anything that might be useful to the case then went to meet Sancha who was descending the stairs with Cyril.

"Nothing interesting up there," she said. "They must have focused their attention on clearing out the office. There are a couple of men's coats hanging in the break room, there's food in the fridge. The coffeepot was cold, so I guess they've been gone a few hours at least. Cyril finished fixing the bathroom so he's gonna leave now. Did you call in a team to collect all the papers?"

"I did—they should be here any minute. Someone's going to draw the short straw and have to piece together that shredding. Let's walk Cyril out then wait outside. Did you fix the problem, Cyril?"

"Sure did. Wasn't a big deal, just a loose connection in the plumbing. I have another job I have to get to so is it okay if I go?"

"Go ahead," Gage said. He watched Cyril leave then turned to Sancha. "I don't think there's much more we can do for the moment, but we should wait for the team to arrive."

She shrugged. "I guess you're right. In fact, here they come." An unmarked van pulled up close by. She and Gage gave the team a quick brief then headed to the car.

"They'll secure the premises when they're done," Gage said. "Best we go find dessert then get back to Treasure Trove. If Landry is cooking, and we're late, my life won't be worth living."

"He sure has you under his thumb," Sancha said, grinning.

"Not denying it," Gage said, grinning right back. As they strolled to the car, he told Sancha about the things he'd spotted. "It does point to this being some kind of jewel trading business. And I'd bet my next paycheck that the reason they cleared out so fast has something to do with the attack on Petey and whatever was stolen from him."

"Not taking that wager," Sancha said. "This case is beginning to stink like that haddock I mentioned earlier."

"You're obsessed with fish. How *do* you know what that smells like? I have questions."

"Nosy detective. There was this one time when my kid brother shoved one between the wall and the radiator in his homeroom. Entire school smelt of rotting fish for months."

"I'm not even going to ask why. Knowing Ernesto, it's the kind of thing he's still doing."

"You're not wrong. That man has a warped sense of humor. He lives to cause mischief."

They picked up the pace and headed into the stream of traffic. One stop for chocolate silk pie, another at the liquor store for Sancha to pick up a bottle of wine and they were outside Treasure Trove before seven thirty. After a quick high five in the car to celebrate their efficiency, they went into the store where Landry was in the middle of cashing up. Petey and Carson were half-hidden behind a bookcase doing something Gage didn't want to investigate too closely. Landry was sticking out his tongue, his brow furrowed in concentration. He held up a hand as Gage approached. Gage shared an amused look with Sancha.

"Don't move," Gage said. "He's adding."

"Then why does he look like he's giving birth?" Sancha whispered.

"He says numbers were created by Beelzebub to torture innocents."

"And Landry classes himself as an innocent?"

"You sound skeptical."

"He's as innocent as you are."

Landry stabbed at his page with his pencil. "Done. You two should be on stage in Vegas by the way. Sooo funny."

"You don't sound like you mean that, honey," Sancha said, holding out her arms for a hug. Landry obliged. "Sorry we disturbed you. Did you lose count?"

"Nah. I have razor-sharp concentration." Gage snorted. "No hug for you, mister."

Gage ignored Landry and pulled him from Sancha's hold. He wrapped Landry in his arms then sucked up a hickey on his neck. Landry melted against him.

Sancha sniggered. "I could sell tickets to people to watch you two. It's like having my own subscription to a private porn channel."

"When do you have time to watch porn?" Gage said. "If you have spare time, you could be doing my paperwork."

"Tell that to my kids, my husband, my cat and the goldfish."

"Oh, honey… Tonight can be your therapy night." Landry patted Sancha's arm. "Food, good company and treasure hunting." Landry took a step back from Gage. "Could you go on upstairs and put the potatoes in to bake? They taste much better if they're done in the oven rather than in the microwave."

"Sure. Just let me go say hi to Carson." Gage left Sancha chatting to Landry while he weaved through the aisles to find Carson and Petey, who he discovered extracting themselves from an adults-only clinch. "Jesus, you two. Get a room." Petey flushed, and Carson gave Gage the finger. "Sancha and I are going up to the apartment to start dinner. Can you hang around while Landry locks up?"

"I'll go outside and do the security grill myself," Carson said.

"Great." Gage caught Petey's quizzical glance. "You'll be much quicker. Landry insists he's an expert at hooking the loop on that thing, but it's a hell of a lot easier for someone who is less vertically challenged."

Petey smirked. "Better not let Landry hear you say that, Gage."

"And you won't be telling him, either, will you?" Carson gave Petey's hair a tug. "Because then I may have to consider punishing you."

Petey caught his lower lip between his teeth and blushed even harder.

"Way to go, Carson." Gage complained. "My ass is grass. I think Petey considers that more of a promise than a threat."

Carson chuckled. "Oh, I do hope so."

Shaking his head, Gage retreated to the cash desk, looped his arm through Sancha's then steered her toward the door to the back hallway. "See you in a few, Landry." Once he and Sancha were on the stairs, he said, "Carson is going to keep an eye on things down there."

"You're really worried that someone might target Petey, aren't you?"

"Just being cautious. We'll talk to the boys tonight, let them know that they need to be watchful. I don't want either of them in the store alone unless the place is full of benign customers. I'd guess one or the other of them goes out for coffee at least four times a day—they keep that café in business. Call me paranoid, but I don't want Landry going through anything like he experienced during the lucky cat affair, and Petey is far too sweet for that kind of trauma. He's been through enough already."

"You realize that both of them are a lot more resilient than you give them credit for?" Sancha waited while Gage unlocked the apartment door.

"You spotted the overprotective tendency, did you?" Gage headed for the kitchen to deal with the potatoes.

"Difficult to miss, what with the flashing neon sign right over your head. Don't worry, I get it. Landry is the love of your life and that dominant streak you have running through you like a seam of gold won't let you countenance any harm coming to him. I'm kind of jealous."

Gage cracked open the bottle of red Sancha had purchased on the way home. "And you are exactly the same about your family. There'd be blood on the walls if anyone tried to harm a hair on any of their heads, and I'm including the goldfish in that group." He handed Sancha a glass.

"I'm now trying to imagine Moby with hair." She giggled and gave Gage a nudge with her hip. "I love you."

"Love you back, partner."

"If we're through with the mutual appreciation session, we'd better get on with dinner. What can I do?"

"Put dessert in the fridge then we can take our drinks through to the couch. If we do anything else and ruin Landry's plans, both of us will be in the doghouse." Gage clinked his glass against hers.

"Sounds like a fine plan."

"Bottoms up."

Chapter Eight

"That was a delicious meal, Landry. Thank you." Sancha rubbed her belly. "My stomach also thanks you." She belched.

"The ultimate compliment, according to Gage. You two spend too much time together," Landry said, snickering. "You're picking up his habits. But now we're all done stuffing ourselves, Petey and I need to put you all to work."

Carson and Petey returned from the kitchen where they'd been doing the dishes. "Were you taking my name in vain, Lan?" Petey waited until Carson resumed his seat before clambering onto his lap.

"Yes. Now focus. We have treasure hunting to do." Gage topped up Sancha's wine glass. He and Carson had stuck to one drink while Petey and Landry had sodas. Landry put his map on the table. "Everyone knows about the map, right? Thanks to Gage we have a new clue — a watermark in the paper. So I thought if we all got to work on the Internet, between us we'd get more information quicker." He produced his sketch of the watermark. "We have the word Bellingham, which could be a name or a place, or even a company. The year 1946 and the outline of a portrait painting."

"I'll take the whole thing as a logo," Sancha said, taking a snap of the sketch with her cell. "I can do a reverse image search and go from there."

"Cool. Petey, can you and Carson check out 1946? Significant events, that kind of thing."

"Sure." Petey bounced in Carson's lap. "This is so exciting!"

"If you don't stop bouncing," Carson said, between gritted teeth, "I'll be carting you upstairs for a spanking."

"Oops, sorry!" Petey stilled. "I'm squirmy. I can't help it."

"Let's relocate to the couch. I may need massage therapy." Carson slung Petey over his shoulder. "Reconvene in half an hour?"

Gage nodded. "No getting distracted."

"I'll go join them," Sancha said. "Leave you guys the table."

"That leaves Bellingham to us," Landry said.

"I'll get my laptop so we don't have to squint at a tiny screen." Gage fetched his machine from the bedroom then set it up on the table. Landry grabbed a notepad and pen.

Gage flexed his fingers, cracking two knuckles. "Okay. Bellingham. Let's see. Names first. Hmm, that's a non-starter, there are far too many results. Let's try places." He tapped away for a while. "This is better. So, there's a place called Bellingham in the UK, another one in Australia and four in the US. One is in South Carolina, another in Minnesota, the third is in Massachusetts, but guess where the fourth is? Right here in Washington. It's in Whatcom County, not far south of the Canadian border, in between Vancouver and Seattle. It's about ninety miles from here."

"The name rings a bell," Landry said, giggling. "It would, wouldn't it? But I don't think I've ever been there. It's an awfully big coincidence that there's a place with that name so close to us."

"It is. So, east of the city are the foothills of the North Cascades Mountains so the terrain is quite steep. Mount Baker is the largest peak at around ten thousand feet. We'll have to look at a topographical map, but I'd guess the contour lines somewhere in that area might match your drawing."

Landry scribbled notes, peering at the screen. "Whatcom Falls Park includes the Whatcom Creek Gorge, which runs directly through the heart of the city. It has four sets of waterfalls and several miles of walking trails. Sounds promising."

"We'll look it up on a map—there's a daily newspaper called the Bellingham Herald. Might be useful for more research if they have an archive."

Putting his hand over Gage's, Landry scrolled down. "Look at this! The place is riddled with mine workings. All this can't be coincidental. The name, the mines, the gorge…it all fits."

"We'll still have to check out all the other Bellinghams, if only to rule them out," Gage cautioned.

"When you get all detectivey, it turns me on." Landry leaned into Gage's side.

"I'll make a note." Gage massaged Landry's neck a little. "Thorough research is important in any case."

"I'd like it a lot if you thoroughly investigate me later on…Sir," Landry whispered.

"That's not up for debate."

"How soon can we throw everyone out without being rude?" Landry fidgeted in his seat.

"We're not throwing anyone out, sweetheart. You'll have to be patient." Gage laid his hand over Landry's groin and pressed, making him gasp.

"So not fair!"

"Life isn't fair. Now, Bellingham, Massachusetts. Not far above sea level, the topography there won't match at all." For the next fifteen minutes, Gage looked up the other Bellingham's they'd found. None of the other ones in the US came anywhere close to being likely matches to Landry's map. Bellingham in Australia turned out to be in Tasmania and right on the coast. It was a tiny place largely made up of shacks used during the summer months, so was easy to exclude.

"Tasmanian devils are kind of cute, though," Landry said.

"Have you been watching cartoons again?" Gage asked.

"Taz is fearsome. I have a pair of boxers somewhere with him on."

"That's nice." Gage went back to tapping on his keyboard.

"It doesn't help my self-confidence when you reject my underwear choices."

"Your underwear is good for taking off, everything else is academic."

"At least it's more exciting than yours. You only ever wear plain black or navy boxer briefs. Not that I don't thoroughly enjoy them, because I do but maybe you could invest in something in leather or rubber…"

"And maybe you could concentrate on what we're doing rather than fantasizing about me in a leather jock."

"Oh my God, you have one, don't you? Have you been hiding wonderful things from me?"

"I'm not saying anything that might incriminate me. Bellingham, England."

"This conversation is not finished."

"Okay, according to Wikipedia, it's famous as a stopping point on the Pennine Way walking trail. Nearby is the Hareshaw Linn Waterfall and the site of early coke blast furnaces. That's quite interesting."

"I love British history so much. Listen to this — it says that within the churchyard on the north side is the Lang Pack, purportedly the grave of a burglar who attempted to infiltrate a local house by hiding in a beggar's pack but was discovered after he suffered an ill-timed coughing fit and was promptly run through with the sword of the house's proprietor. Love it. And the church has connections with a mediaeval cult. This place is fabulous. Nearby there is something called Shitlington Craggs, they have the most unbelievable place names over there. The crag has an average altitude of a hundred and seventy meters. A crag isn't a gorge, though, is it?"

"No, it links to some of the clues better than the other places but nowhere near as closely as the one here in Washington." Gage tapped his fingers on the table. "I don't believe in coincidences. I need to think about this."

Landry yawned, making his jaw crack. "Wow, research is tiring. Oh, good timing, here come the others." Sancha, Carson and Petey joined them at the table.

"How did you get on?" Landry asked.

"Well, there was plenty going on in 1946," Petey said. "But the biggest thing, we think, is that it was when a lot of American soldiers were being repatriated after the Second World War. It took quite a while to get back from Europe. It doesn't really help with our treasure hunt, but then Carson had a brilliant idea."

"It just crossed my mind that perhaps the treasure is something that a returning soldier brought back from Europe," Carson contributed. "Maybe something he shouldn't have had and needed to hide. Who knows what they might have come across when they were liberating town after town."

"That's a really good thought," Sancha said. "I'm afraid I didn't get very far with the watermark. It doesn't resemble any kind of badge or logo that I could find, sorry."

"No, that's interesting too," Gage said. "If it isn't linked to anything then chances are it was deliberately designed by the person who drew the map, so we could be on the right track."

Sancha nodded. "Well, I called a cab and I'm gonna make tracks. It's getting late."

"I could drive you," Gage offered.

"No, we've both had a drink, and I bet you'd rather be getting to bed too. Thank you so much for dinner, Landry. It was delicious."

"My pleasure, any time."

"We'll be making a move too," Carson said. "We'll let you out through the yard, Sancha and wait with you until your cab arrives."

"Cool. I hope your treasure hunting pays off. I'll see you in the morning, Gage."

After everyone had gathered their things, Gage escorted them to the door then locked up behind them while Landry packed up his notes and the computer.

"We didn't scare them off, did we?" Landry asked Gage when he returned.

Gage shrugged. "Don't care. Want you to myself." Landry's face warmed. "Gonna tie you to the bed then do unspeakable things to you."

"Goody!" Landry raced for the bedroom, laughing. Gage caught him before he got there, trapping him against the door frame. He held Landry's arms over his head, pinning him in place. Landry panted, not putting up much resistance. "You got me."

"I did." Gage kissed him, long and hard before carrying him to the bed. "And there's no escape."

Landry stretched out on the bed. "I have no intention of trying to get away. This mattress was worth every cent. It's so comfortable."

"Uh huh. Not thinking about bedroom furnishings right now." Gage proceeded to strip every piece of clothing from Landry's body. Landry squirmed and giggled but was soon naked, his wrists tied to the corner bedposts, his cock standing to attention.

"Spread your legs. Keep them apart and be still." Gage's tone was no longer playful.

"Yes, Sir." Landry spread, raising his hips a little, hoping that the less than subtle hint might encourage Gage to touch.

"That'll get you nowhere," Gage said. "Apart from one step closer to punishment." He sat on the side of the bed, one knee raised, one foot on the floor. He took a loose hold of Landry's cock. "Thought I'd try a little contour mapping. You have some interesting features." He licked a finger then dragged it across one of Landry's nipples.

"Ohhh!" Landry tugged on his bonds but there was no give. He bounced, making his dick jiggle.

"That's not keeping still, is it?" Gage gave Landry's cock a light smack. "Perhaps I should lock this up for a while."

"That's a really bad idea, Sir." Landry froze, hardly daring to breathe.

"I'll give you one more chance but any more squirming and it's forty-eight hours in chastity for you."

Landry worried at his lower lip. "I can't see this ending well."

"All you have to do is keep still for a while." Gage stripped off his shirt. "Not that difficult. Warm in here, isn't it?"

"You want me to look at all those yummy muscles *and* keep still?"

"Yes. Only movement I create is exempt." Gage reclaimed Landry's bobbing erection then began tracing the slopes and valleys of Landry's body. "Contours lines are wide here." He stroked Landry's collarbone. "Slight incline…" Landry's heart pounded as Gage moved south across his chest. "With a couple of high points." Both nipples were treated to a series of hard flicks. Always sensitive there, Landry fought to remain still despite the shocks going straight to his groin. "A nice flat plain leading into an interesting delta." The strokes to his belly were ticklish but as Gage moved lower, every muscle Landry possessed tensed. "Hmm, interesting formations." Gage began fondling Landry's balls. "Temperate climate."

"Oh please, please, please…"

"You're doing so well, sweetheart." From somewhere, Gage had obtained lube. He slicked his fingers then went back to massaging Landry's cock and balls. Landry took short, rapid breaths.

"I'm gonna come!"

"I don't think so." Gage let him go.

"Nooooo!" Landry wailed. "I need to…I need…I…"

"Further exploration required, I think."

"You think bad thoughts!"

Gage hummed. "Wicked, beautiful thoughts." He shucked his pants, doing an odd, wiggly dance to avoid touching them with lube-sticky fingers. Landry couldn't help but giggle.

"Laugh it up, sunshine." Gage wasn't so fussy about removing his underwear and Landry was happy to see how hard he was. He licked his lips, leaving them parted.

"No chance," Gage muttered. "I'm primed and ready to blow and that's not gonna happen until I'm buried in your sweet ass."

"Now you know how I feel," Landry grumbled. "Have you finished map reading, or should I offer directions?"

"Unlike you, I have an excellent sense of direction," Gage said, clambering on the bed to kneel between Landry's spread legs. "What's the symbol for a viewpoint?" He hefted Landry's calves onto his shoulders, shuffling forward until Landry was almost bent double. "Because this is a prime spot for observation purposes."

"Can we finish the geography lesson? I never did manage to work out which was longitude and which was latitude but I know I'm giving you far too much of the latter."

"You're in detention, there's a no-get-out clause. Hmm, this terrain is a little hillier." Gage squeezed Landry's ass. "And this is a textbook example of a gorge." He dragged a finger between Landry's ass cheeks, grazing his hole. "Wow, cave system!"

"Oh my God, stop!" Landry shook with laughter then yelped as Gage gave his backside a sharp smack.

"Not the best angle for a spanking."

"Please fuck me, Sir. My balls are so blue they're gonna be mistaken for giant blueberries."

"They have great blueberries in Maine, did you know that?"

Landry was going to cry or use his safe word, he couldn't decide which but then Gage pressed the head of his cock to Landry's hole. He rubbed more lube along his length, grimacing as he did.

"You need some prep?" He spoke from between clenched teeth.

"No!" Landry yelled, glad that Gage was suffering too.

Gage took him at his word but took his time pushing into Landry's body, his care making Landry warm inside. Gage stilled. "Love this. Love being inside you." He moved in slow increments before building up speed. "You were made for me."

"Oh…" Landry tugged on his restraints in an attempt to focus on something other than his aching cock. Not being able to reach for his dick was the sweetest torture. Gage leaned over him, pushing deeper, pegging Landry's prostate with every thrust. Landry had no idea how Gage had enough grasp on reality to locate Landry's dick, let alone tug it. It was an impressive level of multi-tasking that didn't have to last long because Landry came so fast his orgasm surprised him. He yowled, raising his hips, thigh muscles straining. He caught sight of Gage's satisfied smirk then came all over his hand, sobbing with joy.

Gage didn't let up, as if bringing Landry to completion gave him renewed energy. He came on the next thrust, bottoming out then stilling as his entire body shook. Eyes closed, lips parted... Landry wished he could capture the moment on film.

"Oh my fucking God." Gage took several heaving breaths before withdrawing. He lowered Landry's legs to the bed then clambered to one side, flopping down next to Landry. "That was...better than peach pie."

Landry jiggled his wrists. "Uh, gonna let me go, big guy?"

Gage raised his head. "No." He pushed himself off the bed with a groan, wandered through to the bathroom and returned bearing a dripping washcloth.

"That better not be cold," Landry muttered.

"Would I do that to you?" Gage laid the warm cloth on Landry's belly then proceeded to give him a thorough wipe down, paying far too much attention to Landry's most sensitive parts.

"I'm clean already!" Landry protested.

"Nerves still firing on all cylinders, huh?" Gage's shit-eating grin was infuriating but he stopped wiping. "Just one more thing before I untie you." He launched the washcloth at the laundry hamper before rummaging in his bedside cabinet. "You weren't very good at keeping still. I think I need to incentivize your obedience."

Landry gulped. "I don't like where this conversation is heading." He eyed the device in Gage's hand.

"Clear acrylic. Nice and light. You'll hardly know it's there." Gage fitted the chastity tube with a few deft movements. "There's not even a padlock, it locks with this Alan key."

"Oh good." Landry lifted his head for a brief glance at his groin. He thumped his head back on the pillow. "Technical innovation. That makes all the difference."

"This time tomorrow we'll discuss whether or not it can come off."

"And by discuss you mean you tell me what's gonna happen."

"Exactly." Gage got back into bed, pulling the comforter over them before releasing Landry's wrists from the cuffs.

"So mean."

"I could plug you too, if you like?"

"No, that's okay! Did I say mean? I meant sweet and kind." Landry snuggled against Gage, so his ass nestled against Gage's groin. Gage snuck a hand over Landry's hip to heft the chastity tube.

"If it makes you feel any better, knowing you're wearing this for me will keep me turned on all day tomorrow."

"I'm gonna text Sancha and let her know."

"How long do you want to be trapped in that thing?"

"No texting?"

"No texting."

Landry decided it was a good thing Gage couldn't see his grin.

Chapter Nine

Landry was cooking dinner when Gage got home the following night — all his favorites — chicken casserole with herb dumplings followed by cherry cobbler. "If this doesn't put him in a good, let-Landry-come kind of mood, nothing will." The sound of Gage's key in the door made Landry smile. *All day, I miss him. Knowing he's home safe makes me happy. And horny.* "Hi, honey," he shouted. "Dinner won't be long."

"Hey, beautiful." Gage appeared in the kitchen doorway. He'd taken off his jacket and rolled up his shirtsleeves. "Good day?"

"Frustrating." Landry pouted. "Catch any criminals?"

"Getting close to a few. Can you leave things safely for a few minutes?"

"Sure." Landry turned the burner down underneath the pan of casserole. "Woah!" The world tilted, and he found himself hanging upside down with a prime view of Gage's ass. "Uh, where are we going?"

"Couch." Gage marched to the sitting room where he put Landry on his feet. "More specifically, over the back of it." He grappled with Landry's pants until they and his underwear fell around his ankles. He gave Landry a gentle shove until he was bent over the back of the couch. Before Landry could think up a suitable comment, Gage's hand connected with his backside in a series of stinging slaps. Landry gasped and his cock attempted to swell in its prison.

"What did I do?" Landry howled as Gage spanked him a few more times.

"Don't try to act the innocent with me. You know full well." Gage began fingering Landry's hole.

"Do you have a secret stash of lube in every room? Not that I don't appreciate it, but you seem to be able to open it without making a sound... Which is a tad freaky."

"Quiet, honey, or I'll gag you. I'm giving myself a little reward to make up for an entire day of Sancha taking the piss out of me thanks to your text." Gage proceeded to stretch Landry's channel with deft fingers.

"But I didn't tell her that you were going to spend the whole day with a hard-on."

"Sancha has a mind like a steel trap, Landry. It took her all of thirty seconds to work out what 'Gage may be a little distracted today' meant. When I said no texting, I meant no texting. Zilch, zero, nada."

Landry groaned as Gage nudged at his hole with the head of his very hard dick. "Sorry?"

"Apologies turned into questions don't count." Gage pushed home then proceeded to fuck Landry into a stupor. The pleasure pain of being screwed while he was in chastity blew Landry's mind. He pushed back to meet Gage's thrusts, wailing his frustration and when Gage came, Landry invented a whole dictionary's worth of new curse words.

After planting one final smack on Landry's bare behind, Gage withdrew. "Stay put."

Landry spent Gage's brief absence taking shuddering breaths, not trusting himself to stand upright without Gage's support. When Gage returned it was to push a sizable plug into Landry's ass.

"This will keep my come inside you, make sure you wiggle and squirm through dinner *and* dessert, which will be followed by another night of you locked in that cage." He pulled Landry's underwear and pants up before drawing him into a hug.

"Why do I love it when you tell me off?" Landry asked. "It makes no sense whatsoever."

"Because every now and again you need to be reminded who's in charge. Your need to submit responds well to punishment, especially when you know you deserve it."

Landry snuggled against Gage's chest. "I made all your favorites for dinner to make up for being naughty."

"So you admit it? You knew exactly what you were doing."

"Uh, I think it might be safer if I plead the fifth."

Gage grunted. "Something makes me think I've been played."

Landry batted his lashes and widened his eyes. "I have no idea what you mean."

"Fuckety fuck. Feed me before I get the urge to go find my favorite cane."

Landry extracted himself from Gage's hold then scampered to the kitchen. Canes weren't his idea of a fun time.

By the time they'd finished eating and were snuggling on the couch with mugs of cocoa, Landry was finding it hard not to yawn. "Pineapple, pineapple, pineapple."

"What on earth are you talking about?" Gage asked.

"Someone told me once that if you say pineapple over and over again, it stops you yawning," Landry said.

"I think it's supposed to stop you sneezing, not yawning."

"Now I come to think about it, you could be right. My bad. I didn't want you to think your company was boring me."

"It's been a long day for both of us. I need to talk to you about something."

"Does it have anything to do with Carson hanging around the store all the time?"

"You spotted that?"

"I realize he and Petey are in the throes of first love, and it's all about the passion, but every time I look up Carson's there. I'm guessing you had something to do with that, so tell me what's going on."

"You're right, I did ask him to spend more time at Treasure Trove. I meant to tell you last night when you and Petey were together but between dinner, treasure hunting and mind-blowing sex, it slipped my mind. I'd prefer that neither you nor Petey be left alone in the store at the moment. There's a possibility that Petey might be at risk."

"Is this something to do with one of your cases, or because he got mugged?"

"Both. We think the two may be connected." Gage sipped his cocoa. "An old-school method of money laundering is through the purchase and sale of precious gems. The business Petey was delivering his package to is, or rather was, a jewel trader."

"Was?"

"They've gone. Sancha and I paid them a visit yesterday, and they've cleared out—from the look of things, in a hurry. If the package Petey was delivering contained jewels and the robbery interrupted the chain of the money laundering scam we're investigating, then some very powerful people are going to be interested in anything Petey witnessed. They won't be happy if valuable gems went missing."

"But he didn't see anything, did he? He was unconscious in a dumpster."

"They don't know that. To whoever was behind the robbery, he's a loose end. To those involved in money laundering, he's a potential source of information."

"So the gem traders have made a run for it...why? It wasn't their fault Petey got robbed."

"Do you think the kind of people behind money laundering will care about that? They'll want compensation."

"Oh, I get it. They'll want their money one way or another, but how would they find out about Petey?"

"These organized criminals have sources everywhere. They're like fucking fungus. There were people around when we went to get Petey, then you've got paramedics, hospital admin staff, nurses, doctors, journalists checking into the story, anyone Petey told about what happened... The list goes on."

"Okay, I get the picture, but he's moved here since then, changed jobs, new address..."

"I'm not saying I think anything will happen straight away, but he's hardly invisible and until we solve this case the two of you need to be careful. I'm going to talk to Mr. Lao about cutting the store's opening hours temporarily so that you finish earlier in the evening. I'm not so concerned during daylight hours when there are customers coming in and out all the time, but after dark when it's quiet, it's riskier. I've got a couple of personal alarms for you both, as well."

Landry debated protesting but Gage's protective streak was kind of hot. "Okay."

"What, no smart-mouthed protests?"

"Would I?" Landry snuggled against Gage's chest. "You know best, my love."

Gage spluttered into his drink. "Sucking up to me is not going to get you out of chastity tonight, you know."

Landry pouted. "You can't blame me for trying. But seriously, I would never want anything to happen to Petey, and Carson can't be around all the time. Solve the case quickly, though, I don't like my harmonious existence upset by the criminal fraternity."

"Since when has your existence ever been harmonious? You're made of snark. Cut you and you bleed sarcasm."

"You wouldn't have me any other way. I make your life interesting. Talking of, would you like to take a trip out to Bellingham on Sunday? I'd love to take a look around and see if we can find any more clues."

"Sure, it's not that far, and we haven't been out of the city for a while. I'll do a bit of research and find us a decent place to take a hike. I don't want to leave too early, though, because I was planning to take you to Scorch tomorrow night."

"Ooh, yes please! I can shake my booty in those new latex shorts you bought me."

"There will be no booty shaking. You can kneel demurely at my side and fetch my drinks then I intend to strap you down and give you a nice public spanking."

Landry gulped. In its prison, his cock jerked. He worked the plug in his ass, lips parted, tongue sticking out.

"That's not going to get you anywhere," Gage said. "But watching you squirm is entertaining."

"There's no need to sound so smug," Landry retorted, shifting uncomfortably. "My dick will be searching online for voodoo dolls to get its revenge."

"I wasn't aware your dick was a sentient being in its own right. Regardless, anything it gets up to is your responsibility, and I have no problem keeping it locked up for a really long time."

"It has undue influence over my thought processes. I can't help it. If I don't get to come the self-preservations bits of my brain short-circuit."

"I saw something intriguing online myself. There's a cock cage you can get that comes with a butt plug and urethral sound. Could be interesting."

Landry gulped. "I guess I could suspend his Internet privileges…"

"I suggest you do. Have you finished your drink? I have a really powerful urge to paddle your ass. Can't imagine why."

"Do I get to come?"

"Your innocent optimism is a thing of beauty." Gage put their mugs on the side table then pulled Landry toward the bedroom. "The only bit of you that is innocent."

* * * *

The next day, Saturday, was always busy in the store. Landry had no opportunity to send Petey out for coffee until nearly eleven by which time he had a serious case of the jitters. Petey delivered his extra-tall, extra-hot skinny cappuccino with double chocolate sprinkles, and Landry sank into a battered leather club chair with a sigh.

"It's good to take the weight off my feet for a few minutes." He took a long gulp of coffee while Petey settled onto a padded velvet ottoman next to him. "I'll be sad when we sell this chair. It's so squishy."

"I like when it's busy, and Carson said not to leave you alone unless there were plenty of people around."

"You mean you like all the old ladies fawning over you, and Carson is as bad as Gage. Did he tell you what all this Dommy over-protectiveness is about?"

Petey nodded. "He did. I love how much they care about us and I do like all our older ladies. I never knew my granny, she died before I was born. I need surrogates, and our customers are cool."

"When my grandparents retired they turned into a pair of beach bums and bought an oceanfront place in California," Landry said. "My seventy-six-year-old grandpa still surfs, and my grandmother makes cupcakes with some very dubious ingredients, guaranteed to make the grumpiest person happy." He chuckled. "I aspire to be just like them when I'm old and wrinkly."

"They sound fabulous. I think Carson will age well, don't you? He showed me a picture of his dad and he's a real silver fox. Looks just like an older version of Carson, too. Still has his hair."

"I love that you're thinking about a future with him. You guys are great together."

Petey blushed. "I know we're still new, but it feels right. He's warm and funny and kind. He sees me, you know? Seems to instinctively know what I need. I used my safe word the other day because there was a spider crawling across the bed, and he didn't get cross at all. He stopped everything, took the creepy crawly outside then gave me a long cuddle."

"Excellent domming," Landry said. "Safe words were designed for spiders. I think Gage will stay hot too. I don't think he'll change much, just get grumpier probably. He'll still be spanking me when I'm in my seventies."

"And you'll still deserve it."

"Maybe my gran will give me her secret cupcake recipe."

"Landry! Gage is a cop!"

"He'll be retired by then. How much did Carson tell you about why we need to be careful? I'm not talking about the kind of care that involves latex here."

"He got all serious and stern then gave me a lecture about being alert to my surroundings, keeping an eye out for strangers, that kind of thing. He said it was something to do with a case Gage is working on and what happened to me."

"Gage didn't tell me much more, but I think we should be prepared to defend ourselves."

"What do you mean? I've got no idea how to use a gun and I don't want to learn." Petey shuddered. "I don't like them. They scare me."

"The only gun in this store is that ancient flintlock in the second aisle and that hasn't worked since about 1732. However, there are two sword sticks in the stand near the door so we could move them closer to the cash desk. Somewhere in the bric-a-brac cupboard there's a big jar of glass marbles—we could roll them all over the floor if anyone tries to get you."

"Sounds like *Home Alone 7*."

"Were there that many sequels?" Landry asked.

"Who knows? They seem to be permanently on TV."

"How many *Sharknado* films are there?"

"Uh…five?" Petey wrinkled his nose, deep in thought.

"That's another movie marathon we need to have."

"*Sharknado* or *Home Alone*?"

"Sharks!" They both spoke at the same time. "We got off track," Landry said. "We need more weaponry."

"I know!" Petey sprinted across the store, returning clutching a carpet beater. "This delivers quite a whack!"

Landry snorted with laughter. "We're doomed."

Petey sighed. "We're lovers not fighters."

"Submissives, not subversives."

"Oh, I don't know…you can be rebellious when you want to be."

Landry gaped. "You wound me!"

"And you talk a big steaming pile of horseshit."

The front door bounced open making Landry jump, and Petey gasp. A draft of cold air reached them seconds later.

"It's just Ken, the mailman," Landry said, attempting not to sound as relieved as he felt. He didn't get up. "Hey, Ken. You're late today. It's nearly lunchtime."

"The danged truck had a flat. Took me a while to get it changed over. You two look cozy."

"Taking a break. We've been rushed off our feet all morning."

Ken handed over a pile of mail. "I'll be back on my day off. My mother-in-law loves costume jewelry and it's her seventieth birthday coming up. She wears brooches — maybe you could look out something nice for me?"

"Sure. We have a few. I'm sure we can work out a deal," Landry offered.

"I appreciate that," Ken said. "Gotta run. Some businesses aren't as accommodating as you are when it comes to getting their mail late." He trotted down the central aisle, departing with a wave.

Landry shuffled through the small stack of envelopes. "Mostly bills and flyers. Wait, there's a postcard. I wonder who it's from." The picture on the front of the card was of an imposing building that Landry didn't recognize. He flipped it over. "The National Portrait Gallery, London." The store's address was handwritten in block capitals. On the other side of the card in the message space, there were only two words. "Hide it."

"Who's it from?" Petey took the card.

"It doesn't say." Landry only knew one Englishman likely to send him a cryptic card. "But I'd put money on it being from James fucking Ellery."

"The Brit that got you tangled up with the Yakuza?" Petey asked.

"I'd bet this week's commission on it." Landry frowned. "What does he mean hide it? Hide what?"

"Jesus, Landry, you can be dense. What's the most recent addition to your life?"

"My new lucky cat and the mirror I got from the flea market... Oh! The map. How the hell can James Ellery know anything about that?" Landry's gut churned.

"You should call Gage," Petey said

Landry gave himself a shake. "That can wait until this evening. I don't want to bother him about something so insignificant. He's handling a really heavy case at the moment, remember?"

"Well, when he's beating your ass for not telling him, remember I was the good friend who gave you sound advice, which you chose to ignore."

Landry nibbled on his thumb nail, debating his level of risk. Gage had removed the evil chastity device while Landry was still asleep, and he'd awoken to the heat of Gage's mouth around his cock. He'd come so hard he'd blacked out, and Gage had woken him again by kissing the full length of his body.

"What are you thinking about? Your eyes just glazed over." Petey prodded Landry's arm.

"Believe it or not, I was thinking about taking your advice. I think I run the risk of Gage testing out that carpet beater if he finds out I kept something from him." Landry hauled himself out of the armchair's grip. "I'm gonna text him then start thinking about a good place to hide the map. We're going to need sugar, do you mind going back to the coffee shop?"

"When do I ever mind shopping for baked goods?"

"And more coffee." Landry tapped a message into his cell.

"That goes without saying."

Landry pressed Send and then started counting. He hadn't even got to ten before the phone rang.

"Gage?" Petey grinned.

"No, it's the tooth fairy."

"We have some customers, so I'm outta here." Petey fluttered his fingers in Landry's direction as he flounced down the aisle and out of the door.

"Traitor!" Landry yelled after him. Sighing, he answered the call, holding his cell well away from his ear.

"Is it possible for you to stay out of trouble for more than a few hours?" Gage growled.

"Did you just growl at me?" Landry asked.

"I'll more than growl if you're not careful."

"Ooh, scary... Is it wrong that I'm kind of turned on right now?" Landry kept his voice low and smiled at a customer who was giving him a quizzical look.

"Unless you want to spend the rest of your natural life in chastity, start talking."

"You can't blame me for this," Landry whined. "Blame Ken the mailman. He brought the card."

"Is it signed? Are you sure it's from Ellery?"

"No it's not, and I'm not sure but who else do I know in England? Who else is likely to send me a cryptic message across the Atlantic? Ellery has form, Gage, you know that."

Gage's sigh sounded pained. "Unfortunately, I do. I have questions. A lot of fucking questions. I need to think about this. Are you and Petey safe?"

"As houses. He's out getting coffee at the moment but there are customers in the store and none of them look like axe murderers. It's been busy, plenty of people around and no sign of any nefarious doings." Landry polished his fingernails on his sleeve. "Besides, Petey and I can look after ourselves."

Gage's skeptical grunt wasn't entirely unexpected. "Call me the instant you notice anything out of the ordinary. I'll be home as early as I can. Lock-up when it gets dark, Landry."

"Yes, Sir." Landry gave himself a gold star for keeping sarcasm out of his tone.

"When you're obedient, I get suspicious."

"That's because you're naturally cynical and don't have my sunny disposition. I'm a glass half-full boy whereas you're more likely to ask who stole your drink."

"Go sell stuff. Stay out of trouble."

"Go arrest stuff. Don't get shot," Landry retorted.

"I don't... Never mind." Gage rang off, leaving Landry chuckling and looking forward to the evening of Gage's discipline he'd just guaranteed.

Chapter Ten

Scorch was packed. Saturday nights at the club were always busy, but Landry didn't recall a night when it had been so crowded. It was hot, and Landry was glad for his lack of clothing.

"Sometimes, wearing just a teeny, tiny pair of rubber shorts has its advantages," he murmured from his spot on the floor where he sat cross-legged at Gage's feet.

"Remember our discussion about demure, attentive silence?" Gage gave Landry's hair a tug.

Landry batted his lashes. "I recall a lecture. No discussion took place, Sir, and I'm not good at being quiet."

"No shit."

"Unless you gag me, of course, but that's not fun and it can be drooly."

"I don't spank you anywhere close to enough," Gage grumbled, ignoring Carson's pitying expression.

"That we can agree on," Landry said, tartly.

"It *is* verging on tropical in here tonight," Carson said. "I should have worn less." In his lap, Petey—clad only in a pair of gold cycling shorts — sucked in a breath and blushed to the roots of his hair.

"I think Petey concurs," Gage said. "Me too. Leather wasn't designed for nightclubs, that's for sure."

Landry stroked his thigh. "It's so worth it, though." He walked his fingers closer to Gage's groin. "Especially when it's so soft and tight and tactile."

"I give up. Why don't you and Petey go dance. Work off some of that brat you have going on."

"Yay!" Landry was on his feet in an instant. He hopped from one foot to the other while Petey and Carson engaged in a long kiss.

"Go have fun," Carson said to Petey as they disengaged lips, "Stay where I can see you, though."

"'kay!" Petey bounced, happy as a puppy with a new toy. Landry grabbed Petey's hand then dragged him over to the dance floor. Shimmering heat rose from the mass of bodies already jumping to the beat, and Landry, who normally liked to be in the thick of things, was content to stay near the edge of the illuminated floor.

"We can breathe over here," he shouted at Petey. "And Carson can watch you." He grinned and gestured toward their table where both Carson and Gage were staring directly at them.

"I don't see Gage looking anywhere else."

"Why would he want to when he has all this to ogle?" Landry ran a hand down his bare chest, and Petey snorted with laughter. They danced for a while, bopping happily and holding hands. Landry could sense Gage's constant watch and wiggled his ass in blatant provocation, raising his arms so that his shorts dipped even lower. They only covered the bare essentials as it was, so he was skating on the edge of decency.

"You're gonna be in so much trouble!" Petey mouthed the words. There was no chance of holding a conversation over the pounding music without screaming.

"I hope so," Landry mouthed back, grinning. His smile faded when a big body pressed against his back. He spun around but before he could direct a cutting 'back off' the bearded redhead gave him a rueful grin before slipping into the crowd. Landry spun back to face Petey to find Gage wedged between them, glowering. Carson was at Petey's back, arms wrapped around Petey doing something that was part slow dance part pornography.

"I can't leave you alone for a moment, can I?" Gage stripped off his T-shirt then knotted it into his belt.

Landry shook his head, wishing he had a pocket hanky to mop up his drool. *Holy fuck, I have the hottest boyfriend in Seattle.* He traced a heart on Gage's chest. Gage drew him closer, one hand on each ass cheek, until they were firmly lodged together. He couldn't dance to save his life, but Landry forgave him, accepting the slow grind that created interesting friction in his shorts. He was in danger of coming right there on the dance floor, not that anyone would have cared but it would be gooey and icky and best saved for when they were both naked and horizontal. Gage wasn't helping as he massaged Landry's rubber-wrapped ass, dipping a finger under the clinging fabric every now and again.

"Had enough of dancing yet?" Gage murmured, nipping at Landry's neck.

"I could take a break," Landry squeaked. "Water. Cold water would be nice... Dumped in my lap, preferably. Or I could go ask the barman if I can sit in the walk-in refrigerator for a while."

Gage grabbed his wrist and tugged him from the dance floor, steering him toward one of the curtained playrooms. They weren't private, anyone was welcome to indulge their voyeuristic streak, but they remained curtained off from the wider club audience and dungeon masters controlled the numbers who were permitted to watch.

The space Gage had chosen was empty of people, but in the center sat a spherical frame constructed from aluminum tubing. Gage positioned Landry with his back to one of the curved uprights.

"Lean back, hands above your head and grab the pole."

Landry relaxed his body against the curve, hissing as the cold metal made contact with his sweat-slicked skin. Gage used black bondage tape to bind his wrists above his head while a second piece of tape went around his throat.

"Not too tight?" Gage asked.

The question was academic. Gage was far too expert a Dom to put something around Landry's throat that would affect his breathing. He was held in place, but could sing an aria if he needed to. More tape went around his waist. He was bent in a graceful arc with a view of the black painted ceiling, so when Gage stripped his shorts down to his thighs, Landry hadn't seen it coming. He moaned as the cool metal tube settled between his ass cheeks. He was hard as iron, something that didn't change when Gage bound his ankles to the base of the sphere.

"I thought this might be more fun than a spanking." Gage trailed the strands of a suede flogger across Landry's chest. Landry parted his lips then licked them. He wanted Gage to get started. The anticipation was killing him, and he was desperate to come. He could hear the murmur of voices and knew an audience was gathering. That just made him harder. Bored of the ceiling, he closed his eyes. He wiggled as much as he was able, trying to encourage Gage to get a move on. Needless to say it had zero effect.

"Who's in charge here, Landry?" Gage flicked each of Landry's nipples in turn.

"You are, Sir!"

"Yes, I am and after that display you put on, on the dance floor, I feel the need to exert my authority."

"I didn't do it on purpose, Sir. Okay, I did… But only because I wanted you to watch me."

"Not to draw the attention of every other Dom in the club?"

"No! As if I would do that… It was an unintended consequence of innocent actions." Landry was quite glad he couldn't see Gage's expression because he guessed it would be somewhere between disbelief and amusement.

"Nobody in this entire club would ever describe you as innocent, my love." There was a ripple of laughter from the onlookers.

"I feel attacked," Landry muttered.

"Tell me you're not exactly where you want to be," Gage said. He jacked Landry's cock a few times. "Bound, awaiting my pleasure, watched by a bunch of appreciative spectators." That got Gage a smattering of applause.

"I'm glad everyone finds this so entertaining," Landry muttered.

"I'm not hearing your safe word."

There was no way Landry wanted what was happening to stop. He craved the warmth of the flogger against his skin, the sting that would bring him a rush of endorphins, the knowledge that Gage's attention was entirely his.

"I thought so." Gage sounded smug, confident. "Gonna towel you off a bit before I start." The rough towel not only served to wipe away perspiration, it also sensitized Landry's skin, setting his nerve endings tingling. He anticipated the first blow of the flogger from the air moving against his skin. Gage began with soft strokes, targeting different parts of Landry's body in an apparently random order. Heat built slowly. Occasionally, a bit more weight would cause a sting to a thigh, a nipple. Gage worked the flogger a little harder, and Landry's breath grew ragged. He floated, absorbing the pain. He rubbed his crack against the metal pole. No longer cold, it had absorbed the heat of his body. His cock bounced and the very tips of the flogger caught his shaft. He screamed and at the same time Gage squeezed his balls. Landry came with a jubilant shout, and Gage helped him ride the wave of a juddering orgasm until he sagged in his bonds, exhausted and drained. On the edge of his awareness, he heard voices congratulating Gage, but they faded until he was sure that he and Gage were alone.

Gage peeled the bondage tape away leaving the piece around Landry's waist until last so that he didn't collapsed to the floor. When that was gone, Gage was ready with a hug and a soft blanket. He sank to his knees bringing Landry with him, cradling him, stroking his hair. Landry didn't know or care what he was saying just that he was there and that he was safe in Gage's arms.

"I think you may have to carry me home," Landry murmured, when he had recovered a little.

"I've ordered a cab to haul your lazy ass home. It should be here in ten minutes or so."

"Ten minutes is good." Landry sank lower, groping for Gage's zipper.

"You don't have to." Gage stroked his shoulder.

"Try and stop me," Landry muttered. He freed Gage's cock, which was hot, the tip slick with pre-cum. Landry took it into his mouth, ducking his head until Gage's pubic hair tickled his nose. He sucked hard as he drew back then plunged down again until Gage's shaft hit the back of his throat. He swallowed and Gage came, the hot spurts coating Landry's tongue as he lifted his head a little. Gage wound his fingers in Landry's hair, holding him in place until he was done, then cuddled him close.

"Thank you."

"Very much my pleasure," Landry murmured, still floating. "What happened to Petey?"

"They watched us for a while then Carson took him somewhere private. Carson will bring him home when they're done doing whatever it is they're doing. You, I want in our bed, impaled on my cock."

"Sweet talker," Landry giggled, pulling his blanket closer.

"You want chocolates and roses or another orgasm?" Gage grumbled.

"You should know better than to make me choose between chocolate and something else," Landry said. "But on this occasion, I'll take the orgasm, please.

That's not to say that I wouldn't appreciate the occasional bunch of flowers…"

"So demanding. Gonna gag you later then fuck you until can't walk."

"Is the cab here yet?" Suddenly, Landry couldn't wait to get home. He wanted Gage's arms around him and his cock deep inside him.

* * * *

The next morning, Landry was regretting some of his life choices as he curled into the passenger seat of Gage's Jeep, clutching an extra-large latte like a lifeline.

"Why did you keep me up so late?" he whined, breathing in the aroma of life-restoring caffeine.

"I didn't hear you complaining at the time," Gage said.

"That's because you gagged me."

"And those minutes of blissful silence, were wonderful. Those little squeaky noises you started making were great too."

Landry sighed. "It's not fair. Why do you look like you had a straight eight hours' beauty sleep while I look like I've been dragged through a field by a herd of stampeding wildebeest?"

"Giving you a thorough fucking is as good as a rest to me. It was a good night. That scene at the club was hot as hell then you got all clingy and cuddly in the cab, which was cute."

"You give the best after-care," Landry admitted. "Trouble is, it just turns me on again."

"It sure does. Of course, rubbing balm into your backside is pretty good for me too."

A smile played around Landry's lips. "It should be, I have a very cute ass."

"You can nap if you want to. It'll be an hour or so before we get to Bellingham."

"No, I'll just feel groggy if I do that. One more coffee stop on the way should do it."

"You must have coffee running through your veins, not blood."

Landry shrugged. "Works for me. Did you say that the newspaper office will be open when we get there?"

"Yes. I spoke to a nice lady called Edna who's going to meet us there. She's retired but is the key holder in case the alarm goes off because she lives close by. Their recent records are digital, but the older stuff is still on microfiche. She said they don't have the budget to get it all transferred across yet. Because I'm a trustworthy, reliable detective she said she'd leave us to it. She has her grandkids over for the day so she can't hang around with us 'shooting the shit' as she put it."

"She sounds fun! I'm not sure why she thinks detective equals reliable and trustworthy, though — I've caught you stealing cookies so many times. Anyhoo, we should concentrate our research on the years just after the war. We won't have time to go through decade's worth of stuff."

"Agreed. It would be good to take a hike, too. Get some exercise. Check out the terrain to see if it matches your map. I found a trail that seems pretty close."

"Okay, as long as you don't expect me to go scrambling up mountains."

"Scrambling is not involved. Talking of the map, we should discuss the postcard you received. I don't like the idea that James Ellery is messing with your life again."

"That sneaky Brit has his fingers in way too many pies," Landry muttered. "He should stay out of my peach."

"I… That sent my mind in entirely the wrong direction. He's not getting close to your peach pie, sweetheart, and I don't care whether or not that's a euphemism."

"Good. You're my Dom. You should always protect my peach pie." Landry snickered.

"Lord of the BDSM gods, preserve me. I've been thinking about the whole series of events. In hindsight, I don't believe it was accidental that the flyer for the pop-up flea market landed in my in-tray. Nor do I think it was a twist of fate that the old stallholder put the mirror out just as you turned up a second time. I don't know how Ellery did it, but he did. I'm certain of it."

"That's a bit of a stretch isn't it?" Landry took a long gulp of coffee. "He would have had to rely on us deciding to go to the market, visiting the right stall, spotting the mirror…"

"So explain the postcard then."

Landry squeezed the bridge of his nose. "I've got nothing. I hate it when you're right all the time."

"Score one for me. Did you hide the map somewhere safe?"

"I did. I found the best place ever."

"Don't tell me. The fewer people that know where it is, the better. Does Petey know?"

Landry shook his head. "No. He saw the postcard but I'm the only one that knows where the map is." Landry settled into his seat, watching the scenery rush by. For once the weather was good, the sun bright and, though it was cool, it wasn't uncomfortable. Gage had cracked the window a little to give them both some fresh air. It smelt different than in the city. Fresher, cleaner.

"Do you think you would ever want to live outside the city?" Gage asked.

"Nah, I'm a city boy," Landry said. "But my folks are looking to buy a cabin somewhere, a place that the whole family could use. If they do, then having somewhere to go every now and again would be great."

"Where are they looking?"

"Somewhere in the San Juan Islands, I think."

"Wow. Book us in."

"I think we'll have to join a line, but I have sharp elbows, and my mom loves me best. The Viking twins will have to wait their turn."

Gage snorted with laughter. "Your mom loves all her kids equally. She loves me best."

"Sadly, that may well be true." Landry shook his empty coffee cup in disgust. "And I expect you to take full advantage of that favored position when it comes to future weekends away."

"Shaking that coffee cup's not gonna make me stop. You can get a refill once we arrive in Bellingham."

Landry pouted and closed his eyes. Maybe he could manage a short doze after all.

Chapter Eleven

"I want to be like Edna when I grow up," Landry said, scrolling through more microfiche. "Such a cool lady."

"You're only saying that because she brought you hot chocolate with whipped cream and home-made double chocolate chip muffins."

"It's no secret that the way to my heart is through my stomach," Landry admitted, "but that rainbow beret she had on was spectacular and did you see the skull on the top of her walking stick?"

"I did. She seemed like a nice lady."

"She patted your cheek. She thought you were hot."

"She was at least seventy-five, Landry."

"And that means she can't appreciate a fine specimen of a man? Don't be ageist. She's had more time to decide what floats her boat so you should be honored."

"I'm not in the habit of floating boats for old ladies or anyone else. Get back to work."

"Slave driver."

"I learned everything I know about motivation from Sancha."

"Explains a lot, she'd give Genghis Khan a run for his money." Landry squinted into the viewer. "Don't tell her I said that. Bellingham in the late 1940s was not the most exciting of places. A new florist opened on Main Street, there was an automobile wreck involving escaped pigs, a local baseball team got beaten, again. Wait, this is more interesting. There's an article about the local mine opening up a new level and taking on more workers, including... Wait for it... Returning servicemen. Three of them. Royston McKenzie, Kenneth Brown and Albert Everard. Here, look." Landry slid his chair to one side so that Gage could read the story.

"For more than thirty years, the men and horses of the Bellingham coalmines toiled beneath the city, using dynamite and muscle power to carve a labyrinth of passageways through a thick coal seam. It's a bit flowery." He scrolled rapidly. "It says here that one of the men quit the mine after a coal cart rolled over his leg and left him hospitalized for months. There's also a note of a fatality when a worker went down into the mine at the start of a shift to check the methane level and triggered an explosion — that was Albert Everard. There's a picture here from 1947 of workers leaving the mine. It must have been a hard life."

"And dangerous," Landry said. "Edna said the mines closed around 1955, didn't she?"

"Yes. She said there are some signs of the old workings on the trail through the gorge. I think we should go take a look, don't you?"

"Sure. We have our link with soldiers returning from the war, let's see if we can match the trail to the map."

"We need to lock this place up then return the key to Edna. Her house is on the route to the trailhead so we can drop it off on the way."

"I wonder if she's done any more baking," Landry murmured as he made his way to the door.

Edna Garrity's house was on a large corner plot on the edge of town. Laughter and music came from her yard. Landry followed the noise and the scent of barbecue to find her ensconced on a swing seat surrounded by a rabble of small children. Other adults lounged around the messy garden, which displayed a profusion of flowering shrubs that had no particular design but somehow worked. Even in spring there was a riot of color and scent. A huge weeping willow sat in one corner while a bright yellow-painted summerhouse squatted in another.

"Landry, Gage!" Edna shouted. "Grab a plate, come join us." Curious glances became welcoming smiles as Edna's family gathered round to say hello.

"Thank you, ma'am," Gage said. "That's a kind offer but we're heading out to hike the trail. We called in to return the newspaper office key. Thank you so much for opening up for us."

A rapid explanation of what they had been doing was shared between Edna and her relatives.

"So how did your research go? Did you find anything interesting?" Edna asked.

"We found some references to servicemen who returned here after the war and became miners," Landry said. "It sounds like mining was a hard life."

"Indeed." Edna patted the swing seat next to her. Landry perched on the edge. "But people back then were used to hard work and the mines paid well in comparison to other jobs, so I guess folks thought the danger was worth it. I'm sure it felt safer than the battlefields of Europe."

"Do you know if any of the old soldiers stayed here?" Landry recited the names he'd noted. "We found a story that said Albert Everard died in an explosion, but I didn't find any more reference to either of the other men."

"I recall Kenneth Brown married a local girl, but they relocated to Vancouver a long time ago. I guess he's passed but I don't know if he had family. Royston McKenzie, I knew. He spent the rest of his life here and is buried in the cemetery. He didn't make it to a great age, I think his lungs were damaged during the war and the mining couldn't have helped. He passed about twenty years ago. He never married. Looking back I guess maybe he enjoyed the company of men more than the ladies, but back then..."

"We've come a long way."

"We sure have. Though, there's still plenty of dumbasses in this world." Edna cackled. "Are you sure you boys won't stay for food?"

Gage shook his head. "We should be going if we want to follow the trail in daylight." One of Edna's daughters thrust a foil-wrapped package into Gage's hand.

"It's just some barbecued chicken to take with you." She beamed. "Mom frets about anyone not eating properly."

"Well, thank you kindly," Gage said.

Landry hopped off his seat. "Thanks for all your help, Edna."

"You boys come back and visit me again, you hear?"

Landry kissed her cheek, which was smooth and smelled of lavender. "That's a deal."

They said their goodbyes and returned to the Jeep. As they drove toward the trailhead parking lot, Landry spotted a sign for the cemetery. "Why don't we make a quick stop and see if we can find Royston's grave?"

Gage swung to the right and pulled into the cemetery lot a few hundred yards down the road. Surrounded by a low wall and accessed by a simple wooden gate, the graveyard was laid out in neat rows surrounded by well-kept borders and recently mown grass.

"I love the smell of freshly cut grass," Landry said, breathing in the scent. "Even though it tickles my nose."

Gage planted a soft kiss on the tip of his nose in response. "Come on, it looks like the older graves are toward the back."

"It's kind of peaceful, isn't it?" Landry ambled along the row. "Not like the graveyards you see in films. I always think of the one in *Interview with the Vampire*." He shuddered. "That film was only redeemed by the number of hot men in it."

"Do you rate every movie you see that way?" Gage asked.

"Don't you?" Landry danced away as Gage aimed a whack at his backside.

"I only watch movies when I'm with you, and I inevitably get distracted."

That made Landry grin. "Distractions are fun. Oh look, here's Royston." The headstone was simple, polished granite, inscribed with Royston's name and birth and death dates. Above Royston's name was a carved image that matched the illustration in the watermark on Landry's map.

"You see that?" Excited, Landry traced the design with his finger.

"Seems like we're on the right track," Gage said. "Royston must be our man."

"I'm sure this is a representation of a portrait painting," Landry mused. "This is a frame, with a head and shoulders inside it."

"You could be right. Not sure what it means, though."

"The postcard James Ellery sent was of the National Portrait Gallery in London too." Landry dropped to his knees, pushing some of the grass away from the base of the stone. "There's something else here, some letters. XVXVIVXIX."

"Roman numerals?" Gage asked

"Could be." Landry made a note of the series of letters in his pad. "X is 10, the V is five, I is one. We can think about that later."

Gage snapped a picture of the headstone with his phone. "Let's go. I need to stretch my legs."

It was only another five minutes' drive to the trailhead. There were three other vehicles in the parking lot and a couple with two boisterous spaniels were scraping mud from their boots, leaning against the back of one of the trucks. One of the dogs scampered over to Landry, and he bent to pet her until a whistle sent her charging back to her owner.

"Reminds me of you after too much sugar," Gage said, grinning. "Just with bigger ears."

"Please don't tell me you're into puppy play," Landry groused. "Because I'm not wearing a dog mask or panting at your feet. And before you say anything, I'm not kink shaming. Some of those puppy guys are way cute but I do not want a tail sticking out of my butt." He glared at Gage.

"I'll note that down as a hard limit then." He smirked.

"You do that." Landry traded his sneakers for a pair of battered boots. "Don't forget my barbecue chicken."

"*Our* barbecue chicken is safely stashed in my backpack." Gage swung the bag onto his shoulder. "The map says if we follow the main trail for about half a mile, there's a fork to the right which heads through a narrow gorge to a waterfall and that's where some of the old mine workings were accessed. If we keep up a steady pace, I'd guess it'll take us about forty minutes to get to the waterfall."

"Are you measuring that by the length of your legs or mine?" Landry asked. "Because sometimes when we walk together you forget that your stride is about a foot longer than mine. I don't want to be constantly scurrying to keep up with you." He slipped his hand into Gage's. "I think you'll need to keep a hold of me."

"Fair enough. Perhaps I should have brought a collar and leash."

Landry gaped. "If you want me to hike with a hard-on, you're going the right way about it." Gage just chuckled and tugged him toward the start of the trail.

It proved to be a well maintained, level path, which began to climb steadily after a few hundred yards. The arch of trees above them had kept the ground relatively dry and the leaf mold underfoot was soft rather than slimy. Landry took a deep breath, taking in the scent of pine and sun-warmed foliage.

"If green had a smell, this would be it," Landry said.

"Can colors have smells?"

"I don't see why not." Landry smiled. It was great to be out in nice weather and have Gage all to himself. He had to share Gage with his work, his colleagues, their friends. Today felt self-indulgent.

"Feels good, doesn't it?" Gage squeezed his hand. "To be just us, together."

"Were you reading my mind?"

"Your emotions are all over your face, Landry. You're an open book. It's one of the things I love about you."

"And I love that you know me so well." Landry pressed close to Gage's side. "You understand what I need."

"Most of the time, what you need is discipline."

"And hugs." Landry took Gage's lack of response as agreement. He hummed happy tunes all the way to the point at which the trail split. After that the going got harder and he had to save his breath. After a good fifteen minutes of steep incline, the path levelled out and a few minutes later they reached the foot of a cascading waterfall.

"Oh, wow!" Landry stared at the glittering stream of water. Where the sun caught it, rainbows came and went through the spray. "It's beautiful."

"It sure is." Gage squeezed his hand. For a while they stood and watched in silence. The torrent had to be over a hundred feet high and the noise as the water dropped into the pool below was thunderous. The ground was soaked by the spray, the leaves glistening with diamonds droplets.

"Where's the water going?" Landry asked. Beyond the pool there was no sign of a stream.

"Underground I guess," Gage said. "We must be above the mine workings here. It wouldn't surprise me if some of them were flooded by now. It could be why they were closed. Pumping them out would be extremely expensive."

"I wonder where the old entrance is." Landry looked around but the path didn't go beyond the falls. "Perhaps we passed them already—it's not that accessible here."

"I was keeping an eye out while we walked," Gage said, "but I didn't spot anything. Nature can take a good hold over nearly seventy years." He let go of Landry's hand then skirted the edge of the pool pushing the undergrowth out of the way. At one side of the cascade he clambered up the steep bank then disappeared into some dense foliage.

"Gage, where are you?" Landry followed Gage's tracks in the mud. When he reached the point at which Gage had disappeared, he heard rustling then Gage's head appeared a few meters above him.

"Up here. Be careful, it's slippery."

Landry scrambled up the bank, cursing the amount of mud collecting on his pants. When he got within sight of Gage, he grabbed his hand and Gage hauled him the last few feet.

"You found it!" Landry exclaimed.

"I found something. This couldn't have been the main entrance to the mine. It must have been an offshoot or maybe an escape tunnel, but look..." Gage dropped to his knees and pulled up some clumps of grass to reveal the rusting remnants of rail tracks and the rotting wood of a buffer. "Perhaps empty wagons were stored here." The entrance was completely overgrown, concealed by bramble bushes and ivy.

"There's a small gap," Landry said. "I think I can wriggle through there." He had to lie flat on his stomach then squirm, but once he was passed the dense foliage, the tunnel opened up in front of him and he was able to stand. It was dark, so he used the torch on his cell to illuminate the space. He walked a few meters but then found the tunnel was completely blocked. He had a good look around but apart from a single rusty nail he didn't find anything of interest.

"Landry, get back out here." Gage's urgent whisper had Landry scurrying to return. As he emerged from beneath the bushes Gage clapped a hand over his mouth. "Quiet, I think we were followed." Gage dropped to the ground next to Landry and they both shifted backward into the undergrowth. Landry froze, hardly daring to breathe. Low voices sounded near the base of the waterfall, but Landry couldn't make out what they were saying. Gage pressed a finger to Landry's lips then started to edge forward. Landry wanted to grab him, to pull him back but he stayed absolutely still, terrified of giving away their position. Gage kept moving until Landry's only view was the soles of Gage's boots.

After five agonizing minutes, Gage moved again. "They've gone. It's safe to come out."

Landry squirmed on his belly until he could stand without getting tangled in the bushes. Despite Gage's reassurance, he kept his voice low. "They could have just been hikers, like us."

"I don't think so. I heard them say they must have continued on the main path, 'they' probably being us.

They were following someone, and I didn't see anyone else out here, did you?"

Landry shook his head. He nibbled on his lower lip. "Apart from the people in the parking lot. Do you think they followed us all the way from Seattle?"

"I don't think so," Gage said. "I hope I would have noticed. We get enough training in how to spot a tail. There are plenty of people who could have overheard us talking about our plans for today, at Scorch, in the store, even in the coffee shop. It wouldn't have been that difficult to track us down in Bellingham."

"What about Edna and her family? I would hate for anything to happen to them because of us."

"Edna's not stupid and she has lots of people around here. We can check in on them on the way back, but I'd guess that these guys came straight here. We talked about hiking the trail. I don't recall us discussing going to the newspaper office, though. There were other vehicles at the trail head, they could have been waiting for us to show up or they could have been concealed close by, waiting for us to arrive. We should head back."

"If they've gone, I want to check something out first," Landry said. "There was no sign of anything in the mine tunnel that would give us a clue to the treasure. It looks like it was dynamited to block it off a long time ago. But if Royston is the person who drew the map, and he has to be bearing in mind what was on his headstone, he lived in Bellingham long after the mines closed."

"What are you thinking, Landry?"

"When I was a kid I really loved adventure books and I remember in one that someone hid behind a waterfall, escaping from pirates I think. The way the rock erodes means that there's often a space hollowed out. The waterfall is on the map and it's close to the mine entrance. It's too much of a coincidence. I want to take a look behind it."

Gage looked skeptical. "You're gonna get very wet."

"You don't think I'm going back there on my own, do you?" Landry grabbed Gage's hand.

"Well, fuck, I guess we're both getting wet."

"It'll be worth it if we find something. It's just water."

"I'll remind you of that when you're hiking back down the trail in wet clothes."

"You can always strip me off and wrap me in the picnic blanket for the drive home." Landry blinked.

"Okay, you've convinced me."

"Thought that might tip the balance."

"Let's get on with it. The sooner we're done the sooner I can get you naked and at my mercy."

Chapter Twelve

Gage kept a tight hold of Landry as he skirted the edge of the plunge pool at the base of the waterfall. There wasn't a lot of room to maneuver, and Gage had images in his head of Landry taking a dive into the water. Gage really didn't fancy having to fish him out, or worse go in after him.

"Be careful. If you break an ankle, I'm leaving you here."

"Says the man with the grace of a bull elephant walking on Lego." Landry sniggered then slipped. Gage caught him before he hit the ground and hauled him upright.

"You were saying?"

"Oops. It sure is slippery."

They were within a few feet of the torrent and the spray was soaking Gage's hair and skin. "It seems pretty close to the rocks, Landry. Are you sure we can get behind it?"

"Only one way to find out." Landry ducked through the falls pulling Gage with him.

"Fuck me that was cold." Gage shook himself like a dog, though the quick shower hadn't saturated his clothing as much as he'd thought it might. He glanced around, taking in the greenery-draped stone. Landry was edging his way along a narrow rock shelf less than a meter away from the curtain of water.

"Well, there's no secret cave back here, which is disappointing," Landry said. "My treasure hunting fantasy balloon has been pricked." The rock underfoot was slick. Gage locked his knees then leaned against the limestone, keeping a careful eye on Landry as he did a neat pirouette to make the return journey along the shelf. "There's nothing here." Landry huffed. "Apart from wet, slimy rocks and green slimy plants. Slime is a theme here."

"It was a long shot but worth taking a look." Gage had to turn away from the rushing water, which was making him a bit giddy. Above him, carved into the rock was a familiar series of letters. "I think I found something." He pointed at the spot.

Landry, clinging onto Gage's arm, peered up at the rock. "Oh my God, it's the same letters as on Royston's tombstone. Lift me up so I can look closer."

With a lot of grunting and grumbling, Gage hoisted Landry onto his shoulders, lifting him as high as he could. He braced himself while Landry prodded and poked at the rock.

"There's nothing... Wait! There's a hole behind this moss. Yuck, more slime... I hope there's nothing living in here. What if there's a snake?"

"Hurry up, Landry, you're killing me. If you don't stop squirming you're going to put me in traction, and any snake with a brain will have evacuated when it heard you coming."

"Suck it up, big guy. You have to deal with the trials and tribulations of treasure hunting. There's something in here, but it's stuck." Landry's movements got jerky as he yanked at whatever it was he'd found. Then it suddenly gave way and Landry tipped backward. Gage managed an acrobatic twist out of desperation and caught Landry's sleeve. Landry slithered down Gage's body to land on his knees, at Gage's feet.

"Much as I like you in that position, get up. Are you okay? You nearly sent both of us in for a swim. As it is, I think my spine is a new shape."

Landry got to his feet and made a vain attempt at brushing some of the mud from his clothes. "I'm fine, it came free real sudden. I found this." He held out a rusting tin that looked to Gage like the ancient cashbox that they used to collect cookie money at the precinct. "It's locked." Landry fiddled with the tin but couldn't open it.

"We'll work on that later," Gage said. "We are wet, cold and we still have to do the return walk along the trail and hope that we weren't followed. The tin will have to wait."

"Okay." Landry jumped through the water first then Gage followed, shedding a shower of droplets. He set a rapid pace on the route to the parking lot as much to keep them warm as anything. Landry didn't complain, just strolled along next to him. As if by mutual agreement, they didn't talk. Gage kept his eyes and ears open, scanning between the trees for any sign of the men from earlier. With his nerves on edge, it seemed to take an age to get to the parking lot. He paused in the trees, gripping Landry's arm to keep him still. They had to walk out into the open to get to the Jeep, but it was the only vehicle remaining in the lot. If the people tracking them had been in one of the other cars, they were already gone. Gage wondered why.

"I was expecting them to be here," he said. "If they knew what car we were using, all they had to do was lie in wait." He shielded Landry with his body as they walked across the open ground then wasted no time getting into the car.

"I'm cold." Landry was shivering.

"I'm gonna drive a few miles and find a gas station where we can use the restroom to dry off a bit. I want to make sure we're not being followed."

"Where do you think they've gone?" Landry was rooting around in Gage's backpack, which was in the foot well by his feet.

"I've no idea. Like I said, I expected them to be waiting for us but I'm glad they weren't. What are you doing?"

"I wasn't talking about the men, I'm looking for the barbecue chicken of course." Landry looked at him as if he'd asked the stupidest question in the world.

"I should have known. The package is in the main compartment."

"I'm hungry! Did you have your gun with you while we were out there, Gage?"

"It's locked in the glove compartment. I should have taken it with us."

"We weren't expecting to be followed. We could have taken them, though, right?" Landry spoke around a mouthful of chicken, which Gage had to admit did smell good. "You wouldn't have needed to shoot them."

"Save some of that for me."

"Okay, don't answer my question. I know when you're deliberately avoiding a topic. This chicken is so good."

Gage kept his eyes on the road and gritted his teeth. He was wet, muddy, hungry and grumpy. He was also sorely tempted to pull over, bend Landry over the hood and give him a sound spanking.

Landry, with the open package of chicken still on his lap, fished in the backpack and pulled out the tin that he'd found. Gage estimated it to be about twelve inches long, six wide and six deep. He couldn't wait to see what was inside, but Landry was even more impatient judging by the way he was shaking and pawing at the tin.

"I guess it's locked, but it's also badly corroded around the seal. Choosing the dampest place on the planet to hide it wasn't that great an idea. I don't think Royston was overly endowed in the brain cell department. It's gonna take a crowbar to get this open."

"Well, you shaking it around like a metal maraca isn't going to help any," Gage grumbled.

"You have that little wrinkle between your eyes you get when you have a headache," Landry said. "You want me to drive?"

"It's not a wrinkle, it's a crease," Gage said. "And on what plane of existence would you driving make it any better? It's a headache. You driving would guarantee a migraine if not a mental breakdown."

"You do have a point." Landry shoved the tin back into the backpack. "But in my defense that last incident with the fire hydrant was definitely not my fault."

"You hit it because you were avoiding a squirrel. You'd only been three blocks away to drop off that bureau. It's a darn good job we have friends in the fire department, and I swear every time I see that fucking squirrel it sits there laughing at me."

"It was only a teeny dent," Landry mumbled.

Gage spotted a gas station coming up. "I'm gonna pull in here. Bring the bag, I don't want to leave it in the vehicle."

Gage topped up the tank then went inside to pay and get the key to the restroom. He and Landry dried off as best they could using the hand dryer and paper towels.

"I grazed my knee," Landry said, dabbing at the wound with a towel. "I didn't even notice." He rolled his trouser leg down. "I'm gonna get more snacks, I'll meet you back at the Jeep."

Gage hovered at the door while Landry shopped, knowing that he was being ridiculously overprotective, but not willing to allow Landry to walk back to the car alone. When Landry emerged with a paper sack of junk food, he gave Gage a knowing look. Gage shrugged. "I need to look after you. Sue me."

Landry gave him a brief peck on the cheek. "Love you, you big marshmallow."

"There's no one watching. I could have you hogtied, gagged and in the trunk in seconds and no one would notice."

"Can you save the kinky stuff till we get home?" Landry put an extra sway in his hips as he marched to the car, and Gage followed, with a pained sigh. "And I'm not getting naked, either. I'm only damp and that picnic blanket is scratchy."

About five miles down the road, Gage found a spot to pull over. He left the engine running to keep the Jeep warm.

Landry dug into his paper sack. "I got you some aspirin and a bottle of juice." He handed over the tablets and the drink. "I also got donuts, a bag of chips and some candy."

"I'll take the rest of the chicken," Gage said, reaching for the package. "Thanks for the painkillers."

Landry gave him a shy smile. "I get to look after you too. Submissive's prerogative."

Gage gave a brief nod, but he was touched. "This chicken is great, but we need to eat quickly. I'm really suspicious as to why those guys following us didn't stick around, like they had someplace better to be."

"The map!" Landry exclaimed. "What if they took the opportunity to beat us back to Seattle? The original is hidden at home."

"If that is the case, ten minutes to eat won't make much difference," Gage said. "They'll be a ways ahead of us. Carson said he was taking Petey to his place for the day, so I don't think we have to worry about him being home. I'll drop Carson a quick text to tell him not to go back to the store." Worry showed in Landry's pretty eyes, and Gage was ashamed that he had put it there. "It'll be okay." Gage wasn't too sure that was the truth, but it was what Landry needed to hear. He patted Landry's knee. It worked because within five minutes of them getting back on the road, Landry was asleep, mouth open and snoring. Gage tried to relax his shoulders in an attempt to ease his now throbbing head and hoped that the painkillers would kick in soon. Much to his relief, traffic was relatively light and there were no snarl-ups in the city. He pulled up outside Treasure Trove ninety minutes later.

Landry was still sound asleep, so Gage decided not to disturb him. He looked so young, almost fragile, in sleep. There was mud in his hair and a leaf stuck out from between the blond strands.

He's going to be mortified when he realizes how filthy his clothes are. Gage held down a laugh and snapped a picture with his cell. He slipped from the car, pushing the door closed behind him. Landry didn't stir.

Gage walked down the side of the building to the rear gate, palming his keys. The lock was still secure and there was no sign that anyone had attempted to break-in. Gage let himself in then crossed the courtyard to the door that granted access to the stairwell at the back of the store. He had taken two steps into the hallway when a scrape had him whirling around, but there was nobody there. A fat pigeon had landed in the yard and was pecking away at some unfortunate insect. Gage chuckled, embarrassed at his own paranoia. He decided to check the apartment, make some coffee then return to the Jeep to wake Landry.

Something cannoned into his back, throwing him face first into the stairs. The pressure of cold metal against the nape of his neck made him freeze.

"Stay down, Detective. Don't try anything stupid." Gage had no desire to lose his head and the results of a gunshot at such close range would not be pretty. "Up." He shrugged off the jab to his shoulder. Once on his feet, he twisted to take a look at his assailants. There were two of them, both big, both wearing balaclavas. From their size, Gage thought they could well be the two men he'd seen on the trail in Bellingham. He cursed his stupidity at leaving the gate to the alley unlocked.

"Where's your boyfriend?" Gage couldn't identify the accent other than it didn't sound American or British.

"I dropped him off at the market. I'm meeting him there in an hour." If these guys had been hiding in the alley while he unlocked the gate, they couldn't have seen him pull up or know that Landry was still in the Jeep.

"Nice and easy, you're going to walk up the stairs then let us in to your apartment. Then you're going to give us the map. Cooperate and you'll make that pickup at the market."

There was no point denying he knew about the map. If he led the men to the apartment, Landry would stay safe, and Gage could buy some time. He tramped upstairs, hoping to gain an advantage at some point.

Inside the apartment, everything was quiet. Gage walked to the sitting room where he had more space to maneuver then turned to face the gunman and his associate.

"The map."

"I'd love to help you, but I don't know where it is."

"Bullshit. A shattered kneecap takes a while to recover from. I'll ask you once more. Where is the map?"

"And I'm telling you, genius, I have no idea." Gage had decided that his only course of action was to charge the gunman when he heard a key in the front door. "Fuck, Landry."

"Loverboy didn't take long fetching groceries then."

"Landry, run!" Gage yelled, but it was too late. Landry, sleep tousled and bewildered, appeared in the doorway. Gage made a dive for the gunman but caught a blow to the temple that knocked him to the ground, dazed.

"Give us the fucking map, now!"

"He doesn't know where it is," Landry shouted. "Leave him alone."

Gage watched, helpless as one of the men grabbed Landry then twisted his arm up behind his back. "But you do, don't you?"

Gage attempted to get to his feet but got a kick in the ribs for his trouble and a renewed view of the rug.

"Don't hurt him!" Landry fought the man holding him. "I'll give you the stupid map. It's in the bedroom."

"Go and get it. Bring it back here or your boyfriend is going to gain a few additional holes."

Landry blanched and his eyes glistened. Gage nodded at him. "Do as he says, Landry."

Landry, escorted by the second man, headed for the bedroom, returning a minute later clutching a sizable purple vibrator which he thrust at the gunman.

"What the fuck is this?"

"You wanted the map, it's in there."

Gage snorted into the rug. The kick to his hip was worth it. The gunman threw the vibrator at his colleague who juggled it from one hand to the other with a grimace.

"Haven't you ever seen a sex toy before you sad excuse for a human being? Unscrew it," Landry said. "The map is in the compartment where the batteries go."

"I don't get paid enough for this."

Gage couldn't believe Landry's front. He prayed the gunman didn't lose his temper. With a huff of impatience, Landry grabbed the toy back, unscrewed the base and knocked it against his palm until a role of paper dropped out. "You've got what you came for, so leave us alone." He handed over the map. The man holding the gun took a quick look then shoved it into his jacket pocket.

"Don't follow us."

"You couldn't pay me enough to trek after your sorry ass!" Landry yelled.

"Landry love, please stop taunting the bad men." As soon as they had gone and the apartment door slammed, Gage hauled himself to his feet. Landry threw himself into Gage's arms.

"You're not safe to be left alone, Gage. Are you okay?" Landry touched Gage's temple. His fingers were ice-cold.

"My headache's back," Gage said, giving him a wry grin. "I can't believe you hid the map in a sex toy."

"It was a good place. Who would ever think to look there?"

"I'm sorry you had to hand it over. I can't believe they got the drop on me. I should have been more observant."

"Not much you can do when someone's got a gun in your face," Landry said. "And who says I handed it over?"

"I saw the map…"

"You saw *a* map. I made a copy. Except it wasn't quite the same as the original and of course there's no watermark."

"So where *is* the original?"

"We own more than one vibrator, love."

Laughing hurt. Gage held Landry close. "I need to call this in, but it can wait a few minutes while I hold my ingenious, brave lover. I'm proud of you, sweetheart."

Landry snuggled closer, and for once Gage let him be the one to provide comfort and support.

Chapter Thirteen

"I can't believe you let me nap when we have a tin of treasure to investigate," Landry said, tucking into his second slice of pizza. "I'd already slept in the car."

"Not for long, and we both needed rest. Besides, it wasn't intentional. One minute we were chatting, the next you were snoring on my chest and you kind of lulled me to sleep too."

"I do not snore!"

"You do. Like a puppy."

"Sounds kinda cute. How did it go when you reported our unwelcome visitors?"

"It's on the record, that's the main thing but there wasn't any point in getting anyone over here. They were wearing balaclavas and gloves, so no description and no chance of prints. All I could say was that they were white, one had blue eyes, the other brown and that one had a scar running through his eyebrow."

"You saw all that! I was so scared I couldn't even say what they were wearing."

"You didn't come across as scared, you seemed mad."

"That was reaction to terror. My inner snark surfaced because they wanted to hurt you."

"When I'm back at work I can get CCTV footage pulled to see if we can identify their vehicle but it'll no doubt turn out to be a rental or stolen. Our chances of catching them are minimal."

"I suppose you're right, though I'd rather they were both thrown in a cell and given the same treatment they gave you."

"Wow, feisty! We don't do that, you know."

Landry shrugged. "I'd help. Pizza was the best idea you've had in a long time. Stuffed crust is my favorite." He licked his fingers. He and Gage were seated at their dining table, dressed in their pajamas, with cans of soda and a large open pizza box. Next to that sat the Bellingham tin, as Landry had named it. Gage had already rubbed around it with some wire wool to get rid of as much of the rust as possible and now he had his Swiss army knife open and was attempting to insert the blade into the join between the lid and the body of the box.

"I'm seeing a whole new side of you."

"I'm a man of many layers," Landry said. "My violent layer is buried deep—like Mariana Trench deep."

"Look at you with the deep-sea references. This is definitely easing," Gage said. "I'll have a go at picking the lock."

"You can do that?" Landry discovered new admiration for Gage's talents. "That's so cool. I can use you in the store to open things that come in without keys."

"I've picked up a few skills here and there." Gage probed the keyhole with a spiky tool. "These boxes are designed to be particularly secure, but the mechanism is rusted." Landry drummed his fingers on the edge of the table. "Stop that. It won't help me do this any quicker."

Landry sat on his hands. He couldn't wait to see what was in the tin. "I'm imagining gold bars and jewels and treasure!"

"Well keep that imagination of yours under control, because I don't think the tin is heavy enough for any of that."

"A boy can dream."

"What you think of as treasure and what constituted value to Royston are most likely to be different things. Got it!" There was a grating click and the lid of the tin flew open. "You can do the honors." Gage pushed the tin in front of Landry.

Landry couldn't immediately see anything because the contents of the tin were wrapped in a soft cloth. Carefully, he unfolded the top layer, spreading it out. He lifted several items from the tin and laid them on the table.

"So, we have some medals, I guess they're Royston's from the war. Letters bound in a blue ribbon. A faded newspaper clipping and a book of nursery rhymes." Landry lifted the cloth to check underneath it. "Oh, look!" A tarnished coin sat in the corner of the tin. Landry picked up the coin, which was black with dirt, to take a closer look. "It's a twenty-dollar coin," he said. "That would have been a lot back then. I can see the date, 1927." He added it to the pile of treasure.

"The newspaper clipping is interesting," Gage said. He handed it over.

"Nazi art theft," Landry read. "There are very few known Raphael self-portraits, and scholars believe that one may be *Portrait of a Young Man* — circa 1515 — which was acquired by the Czartoryski family in Poland in 1800. Afterward, it was put on view at the family's museum in Krakow. But during World War II, the painting disappeared, along with hundreds of other pieces that the Nazis took from the family's cellar as loot." Landry exchanged a look with Gage. He gulped. "Briefly, there was hope that it had been found — reports in 2012 claimed that the painting was located, though these were quickly debunked. For now, an empty frame that once held the canvas is on view at the National Museum in Krakow. That's so sad. Imagine going to see an empty frame."

"If that is Raphael, he was pretty," Gage observed gesturing at an image of the missing portrait. Landry glared. "Not as pretty as you, sweetheart."

"Nice save. And he'd be over five hundred years old by the way, so icky!"

Gage yawned. "Sorry, I'm flagging and I have to be at work at the ass crack of dawn "

"Mondays are often quiet in the store," Landry said. "I'll start researching all this stuff and we can reconvene over dinner tomorrow night. I can't wait to find out more about Royston's life."

"You're not disappointed?"

"No! I think this odd collection of stuff is going to lead us to bigger and better things."

"I'm going to see if I can find a way of getting in touch with James Ellery. He's been manipulating this treasure hunt from the start. I'm convinced of it, and he doesn't do anything unless it benefits him. If there's a

Raphael painting at the end of all this, his involvement makes much more sense."

"So cynical, so sexy." Landry grabbed Gage's pajama top and pulled him down for a kiss. "But I agree. I feel like a puppet, and he's holding the strings."

Gage hoisted Landry into his lap. He began to fiddle with the ties on Landry's pajama pants.

"And nobody gets to play with your strings except me."

* * * *

If Landry dreamed, he didn't remember. Gage had summoned up enough energy to give him a thorough, enthusiastic fucking, and they had both fallen asleep immediately afterward. Landry awoke rested if a bit sticky and the bed next to him was already cold. Gage had left a note next to the coffee pot where Landry was guaranteed to find it, which just said 'be careful' next to a little heart.

"Aw, he's such a cutie." Landry traced the heart with the tip of his finger. "Could have woken me up with a mug of coffee... But no man is perfect." He went through his morning routine and even had time to strip the bed and throw in a load of laundry. The washer and dryer were housed in a utility cupboard in the basement and were shared with Petey. Landry rescued a single red sock from the washer just in time, cursing Petey's name. Gage would not be amused if all his white clothes turned pink. The near miss didn't deflate Landry's good mood and he bounced into the store, travel mug in one hand and the Bellingham tin in the other. Petey was already there, dusting near the front of the store.

Landry dangled the sock in front of his face. "Do you know how dangerous one of these can be? I narrowly missed a humongous disaster when I put our laundry in the washer just now."

Petey gave him a sheepish grin as he grabbed the criminal sock then stuffed it in his pocket. "Sorry. I was wondering where that had gone. Why is it that pairs of socks go into the washer but never come out? I've lost count of how many odd socks I have." He held up one foot, then the other, revealing that he was wearing one blue and yellow striped sock and one yellow one with white polka dots.

"You could start a new trend. Stop that dusting because I've got loads to tell you."

"Let me just turn the closed sign to open," Petey said.

Once Landry had set up the register and opened the purchase log to a fresh page, he and Petey dragged two chairs behind the cash desk. "We need to put out no customers vibes," Landry said. "Because we don't have time to make sales today."

Petey giggled. "Then you're shit out of luck because Mr. Abner is about to walk in."

"If he wasn't such a sweet old guy, I'd curse."

"You were the one who tempted fate by saying you didn't want any customers today, it'll be non-stop now, you realize that?"

Landry spent half an hour dealing with Mr. Abner, who had good taste and a bottomless bank account. He adored rare books, and Landry had kept several back for him to look at. He loved all of them and left happy as a pig in muck. Landry resumed his seat and waited for Petey to finish with another customer.

"Finally. I'm more frustrated than when Gage puts my dick in a cage. Oh, that rhymes. I've created a new genre—chastity poetry."

"I wouldn't mention that to Gage," Petey said, "or he'll be giving you motivation for a few more verses."

"Good point. He does have a peculiar obsession with putting my cock in prison. I guess it's the cop thing. Incarceration is his watchword."

"Are you going to tell me about your day out, or are we going to spend the day discussing Dommy habits like we usually do?"

"For once, I have interesting things to tell you about other than kink."

Landry spent the next hour recounting the events of the previous day while Petey listened, eyes growing wider by the minute.

"Unbelievable. It sounds like an adventure story, but I would have been so scared."

"I was too but I knew Gage would take care of me, you know?"

"What on earth have you got yourself into? Or, more to the point, what has James Ellery got you into?"

"I don't know, but the mystery is getting more complicated. The good thing is we have the tin and plenty of things to investigate."

The tin was on the shelf under the cash desk. Landry glanced toward the front door. They hadn't had a customer for the last hour. The rain was bucketing down outside and there was no sign of an imminent interruption. He pulled the tin onto his lap so that it couldn't be seen if anyone came in.

"It's a weird collection of stuff," he said, handing the book of nursery rhymes to Petey. "I understand the medals, those we need to check out online and see what they were given for. I haven't had a chance to read the letters yet but there are only three and they are addressed to Royston care of the vicarage in Bellingham, England. Then there's this." He handed over the newspaper clipping.

"I've read about this before," Petey said. "There were some rumors a while back that it had been found, but they were discredited. It's a beautiful picture."

"I didn't know you were an art fan."

"Raphael isn't really my thing. I prefer the Impressionists," Petey said with a dreamy smile on his face. "One day I want to go to Giverny to see where Monet painted."

"He was the one that did all the pretty waterlilies, wasn't he?" Landry asked. "My mom has a print of one of his pictures on the kitchen wall back home. You know there's a book on the bottom shelf over there, one of those giant coffee table things with loads of his pictures in." Landry ran to get. He brought it back and handed it to Petey. "You should have it on *your* coffee table."

"I can't afford this." Petey stroked the book.

"It's a gift from me," Landry said. "And don't argue with me, Petey, because I'm your boss."

"Thank you. I love it. I'll look at it properly this evening." Petey slid the book under the cash desk. "Was there anything else in the tin?"

"Just this." Landry handed over the coin. "Something else to research. I don't know anything about coins. It's not something we've ever stocked."

"If it's rare, it could be valuable," Petey said.

"Or it could be worth the twenty dollars face value. I don't know why an ex-serviceman who became a miner would have something valuable and just hide it.

He could have used the money, I'm sure, if it was something saleable."

"I guess so. It must have meant a great deal to him for him to hide it, though."

"It's on the investigation list. There's something else, well two things actually. I forgot to mention that on Royston's headstone in the graveyard, there was a carved image of a portrait the same as the one in the water mark on the map. There was also a series of letters that we also found carved into the rock behind the waterfall."

Landry wrote out the series of letters that he'd copied into his notebook.

Petey stared at them. "Roman numerals?"

"Could be, but they don't seem to make much sense."

Petey's eyes lit up. "I'll have a go at deciphering it. I love puzzles."

"My best friend is a geek," Landry muttered.

"I'm gonna get you that on a T-shirt," Petey retorted. "You're definitely on the right track with the treasure map. How long do you think it will be before the men that attacked you and Gage last night realize they haven't got the real map? That hiding place was inspired by the way."

"Wasn't it? There's no reason they should. I did a pretty good forgery, even if I do say so myself. If they test the paper, it dates to the late thirties. I took it from an old book that was falling apart. Mr. Lao has taught me everything he knows about spotting fakes. So I knew what not to do. The map was similar enough to the original to be realistic, I based it on the topography in Bellingham. They already know we went there so I'm not giving anything away, but what I did could be matched to dozens of other places."

"Then let's hope they don't come calling."

"I don't think they've got any reason to. I've talked your ear off this morning, you haven't told me what you and Carson got up to yesterday. Did he show you a good time?"

When Petey blushed, he did it in style. His cheeks reddened, his neck got blotchy and even the tips of his ears went scarlet. Landry would bet that he was bright pink under his clothes too. "That good, huh?"

"He has a really nice place. His dad came from money and his grandparents set him up with a trust fund when he was born. He doesn't need to work but became a firefighter because he wanted to make a contribution. He has a house with a garden and he's built this cabin on his land and installed a playroom."

"Oh, wow. That sounds amazing."

"He showed me everything, but we didn't play. He said he wants to take things slow with me, learn what I like. He says we have time to get to know each other properly. He's so different from the other Doms I've met, Lan."

"You're falling for him." Landry grinned. "I'm glad, he's a keeper."

"I am really scared of getting too close. What if it doesn't work out? He's so… It's just that all the subs at Scorch think he's amazing. What does he see in me?"

"Sweetie, if I could give you a transfusion of self-confidence, I would. You have nothing to worry about. I'm pretty sure that no one would buy pure silk ropes to tie you up with unless he thought it would make you happy."

Petey blushed even more. "They were pretty colors too. I'm gonna work on these numerals now."

"Okay, but we are going to revisit this topic of conversation. Frequently."

"I'm sure." Petey grabbed a pad and pencil then escaped to the other end of the store, settling onto a chintz-covered chaise-longue that Landry couldn't wait to get rid of.

Landry grabbed the book of nursery rhymes to have a look through. He checked for any markings or writing that didn't belong but didn't find anything. It had a board cover and the colors were kind of faded. The publication date was 1942. It seemed to have been designed as an early reader for a child because it contained just six rhymes in large print. Landry was familiar with Humpty Dumpty and Little Miss Muffet. Hickory Dickory Dock he didn't remember at all, but he could recite Jack and Jill. Ding Dong Bell was vaguely familiar, and he could remember his mom singing Twinkle, Twinkle, Little Star to him. He read through all the lines twice, but nothing jumped out as a clue. He even checked all the book's seams and creases in case there were any hidden compartments, but the book was completely benign. Puzzled, Landry put it back in the tin then pulled out the sheaf of letters. He untied the ribbon, which was stiff with age and began to read, keeping half an eye on the door. The contents of the letters were mostly identical. Each was addressed to Royston, but there was no date. They were only signed with an initial, which could have been an I, J or T and made cryptic references to keeping something hidden. The something wasn't described. "I know what we did was wrong," Landry read. "Keep it hidden. This shouldn't come out until long after we're gone. No one should benefit from the horrors of the past." Each letter, written in neat copperplate handwriting, in faded blue ink, said the same thing albeit in slightly different words. Landry read them all again, feeling the anxiety of the writer in every word. Whatever Royston and his correspondent had done, at least one of them had regretted it. That Royston had kept the letters suggested that he felt the same.

"The mystery deepens." Landry put everything back in the tin then shoved it to the rear of the shelf under the cash register, tucking his jacket around it. He had to spend at least part of the day justifying his salary and there was work to do. He left Petey to his puzzling and set about finding some good pieces of costume jewelry to put aside for the mailman.

Other than a brief, heart-pounding moment when a motorcycle courier dropped off a package and didn't remove his helmet, the day proved to be uneventful. Landry found time to read through the nursery rhymes again and do a bit of research into their background. He was horrified by the often grim history behind them. He read through the letters again too, remembering to hold the paper up to the light to check for watermarks, but remained frustrated by his lack of progress. He locked up early, as Gage had arranged with Mr. Lao, then he and Petey settled down to review their research. Petey was buzzing with excitement.

"It's taken me all day, but I think I finally worked it out. Literally, five minutes ago I had a jolt of inspiration. If you take the series of letters individually and assume they are Roman numerals, they don't make any sense, at least nothing I could work out. But, if you group them together, like this..." He showed Landry a page of his pad, which was covered in scribblings. "XV XVI V XIX, that's fifteen, sixteen, five, nineteen."

"I think my brain cells have definitely dissolved," Landry said, "because that's not making any sense."

"I didn't think so either but then I thought I shouldn't take the numbers at face value. I think it's a simple code. If you match the numbers to the letters of the alphabet you get O P E S."

"Opes? Call me thick, but I don't think that's a word."

"Not in English it isn't, but in Latin it is. I put the word through a translator, testing it in different languages. Guess what it means in Latin, Lan."

"It means smack your friend around the head so that he stops teasing."

"Well, like most Latin words, it's open to some interpretation, but its main meaning is wealth. It can also mean treasure."

Landry gaped at his friend. "Oh. My. God. That can't be a coincidence, can it?"

Petey shrugged. "I don't think so, do you?"

Landry threw himself onto Petey to give him a bear hug. "You're a genius!" The hug turned into wrestling and tickling until both Landry and Petey were howling with laughter.

"What in the ever-loving heck are you two doing?" Landry extracted himself from Petey's grip, rolled onto his back with his head in Petey's lap and stared into Gage's blue eyes.

"Something you to want to tell us?" Carson stood next to Gage, arms folded, pecs bulging.

"We were celebrating Petey's code breaking skills," Landry said, blowing the hair away from his eyes.

Gage shook his head. "You're supposed to be staying alert. What if it hadn't been Carson and me coming in?"

"The front door is locked, the security shutter is down and Mr. Lao is the only other person with a key." Landry sat next to Petey and attempted to tidy his clothes. "Did you bring food?" He eyed the take-out bag Gage was carrying. "Smells yummy."

"Carson called me at the end of his shift, and we agreed to meet up and get Thai food on the way back."

"I approve," Landry said. "We should have a shop picnic."

"That would be so fun!" Petey jumped into Carson's arms, wrapping his legs around Carson's hips.

"Then that's what we'll do, cute stuff." Carson and Petey started kissing.

Gage rolled his eyes. "I guess that leaves us to move the furniture then."

He and Landry shoved enough seats together behind the cash desk that they could all sit around a low steamer trunk. He laid out the food and unwrapped several sets of chopsticks while Landry found a stash of paper napkins. By the time they were done, Petey and Carson had finished sucking face and joined them. Petey was flushed and there were several hickeys marking his neck. His eyes were drugged and glassy.

Landry laughed. "I'm glad you two came up for air. The food will get cold." Petey squirmed his way onto Carson's lap, grabbing a carton of noodles. "If we're really unlucky," Landry said to Gage, "they'll start re-enacting that scene from *Lady and the Tramp*."

Gage snorted with laughter. "How about you tell us about your code breaking, I assume you've been exploring the contents of the tin today."

"In between customers, yes. I looked at the letters and the book of nursery rhymes. The letters make it clear that Royston was hiding something, and they were addressed to him in Bellingham, England, so he must have gone there on the way back from Europe when he was being repatriated. They don't mention what he was hiding but the letters reek of guilt. The fact that there's a newspaper clipping about a missing Raphael portrait in the tin, something that everyone assumes was stolen by the Nazis, makes me think that Royston and whoever was writing to him somehow got their hands on it. The portrait was the shape of the watermark on the map, and it was also on Royston's headstone. It definitely wasn't hidden with the tin behind the waterfall and that's a good thing because it would have been ruined in the damp, but there doesn't seem to be any indication of where it might be." Landry shoveled more food into his mouth, wow this nasi goreng is amazing."

While Landry ate, Petey took over the story and explained how he had deciphered the code from the numerals Landry and Gage had discovered on the headstone and seen again behind the waterfall. "But the word itself, doesn't get us anywhere. It's just one mystery after another."

"The only things I haven't had a chance to look into yet, are the coin and the medals," Landry said. "They could be unconnected. They may just be things that meant something to Royston, but I still need to check them out."

"You've been busy," Gage said. "You'd make a good detective." Landry beamed. A compliment from Gage meant more to him than anything. "You still need to be more aware of your surroundings. That goes for both of you."

"So stern." Landry shivered. "We should play student and professor tonight." He pressed the heel of his hand against his rising cock. Gage's cheeks were a little flushed and he swallowed, making his Adam's apple bob. "Petey can finish closing up."

"I do need to teach you something about self-preservation. I think you'll absorb the lesson better with a glowing behind, don't you?"

"I always did learn better through demonstration." Landry licked his lips then whooped as Gage hoisted him over his shoulder and made for the stairs. Petey and Carson's laughter following them.

Chapter Fourteen

At the precinct the next day, Gage leaned back in his chair and let his mind drift while Sancha went to fetch them both another mug of coffee.

"Someone got laid last night!" one of his colleagues yelled from across the room. Gage realized too late that he was grinning. He gave the other detective a slow smile and the finger. "Fuck off, Carmichael. At least I'm getting some and not ordering life-sized inflatable dolls from eBay." His gesture was returned but nothing could alter his good humor. He was a little tired, but Landry had pressed all his buttons the previous evening, throwing himself into the role of a student who'd missed the deadline for his latest assignment and was prepared to do anything for a good grade.

Gage, playing the strict professor, had offered a sound spanking and followed through after stuffing Landry's mouth with a ball gag to prevent anyone else on the faculty discovering them. He finished off with two strokes of his cane, leaving a pair of beautiful, parallel lines across Landry's backside. He'd then bent him over the dining table and given him a fierce fucking for coming without permission. Landry had come up with a number of further excuses for why his work was always tardy, getting increasingly inventive as the evening went on. The dog hadn't just eaten his papers, he'd buried them in the garden alongside his bone... Landry had stayed up all night nursing a sick relative who'd overindulged at an oyster bar and swallowed a pearl without noticing... He'd had to leave his assignment in the trunk of his car because a passing Canada goose had hopped in and those things were evil incarnate... It had taken every ounce of Gage's willpower not to break down laughing and hold onto his character. It had been a fun evening, made complete by some entirely vanilla lovemaking in their bed and a lot of cuddling. Gage sighed. *I am a very lucky man.*

"Get your mind on the job, partner." Sancha thrust a mug of coffee at him. "My usually sunny disposition has been darkened by whichever idiot finished the coffee and didn't make a new pot. If I find out who it was" — she raised her voice, getting the attention of everyone in the room — "he's going to wish he was spending the day on traffic duty on a nice congested highway somewhere, sucking down exhaust fumes."

There were several audible gulps. Gage shook his head. "What a bunch of chicken-shit detectives, peeing their pants every time you get loud."

Sancha preened. "They should be scared, too." She glared at anyone who dared to make eye contact.

"This is excellent coffee, Sancha." Gage raised his mug in a toast.

"Nice self-preservation technique, Roskam. Now, if you've finished daydreaming about Landry and whatever the two of you got up to last night, could we do some actual police work?"

"I want to have a go at identifying these first," Gage said, laying Royston McKenzie's medals on the desk. "And see whether or not we can find out anything about his military background. Landry said Mr. Lao is delivering a whole load of new stock today so he's not going to have time to do any more research. Considering the lengths someone is prepared to go to, to get hold of Landry's map, I want to get this research done as quickly as possible. We need to get to the bottom of this treasure hunt."

"Well, you experienced a home invasion. We can contribute to the investigation, so it counts as work even if it's not strictly our day job. I'll get in touch with a contact I have in the military and see how we go about researching McKenzie's background. You take the medals."

"Deal. Thanks, Sancha. I appreciate it."

They both tackled their phones and computers. Several cups of coffee, two cherry Danish and some bagels later, they agreed to share their results.

"I worked miracles for you, Roskam. You owe me big time and by that I mean taking the rug rats out for a day so Pietro and I can get down and dirty. Nearly sixteen million Americans served in uniform during World War II. According to my contact, The National Archives and Records Administration has custody of many of the records relevant to personal participation in the war. It would be a lot easier if we could get our hands on a copy of McKenzie's discharge form because all veterans received a brief, single page summary of their service. It covered things like rank, service number, dates of service, unit, battles and campaigns and decorations and awards—but we don't have that. The National Personnel Records Center has custody of the personnel files for individuals who served in the army, but a fire destroyed eighty-five per cent of the army's individual files in 1973."

"Fascinating. So, did you get anywhere?"

"Patience, big guy. Am I the best detective you know, or not?" Sancha buffed her fingernails on her blouse.

"Yes, Sancha. You are the best detective on the entire planet, bar none. Poirot, Sherlock Holmes, Columbo… None of them are a patch on you."

"I detect no lies. I found out that some veterans may have had their forms recorded or registered at County courthouses, so I called Bellingham and bingo."

"Are you gonna tell me, or do I have to play twenty questions?"

"McKenzie was in the 12th US Army group, 90th infantry division. On the fourth of April, 1945 elements of that division found a sealed salt mine containing a large portion of the German national treasure. It included vast quantities of German paper currency, stacks of priceless paintings, piles of looted gold and silver jewelry and household objects, and an estimated two hundred and fifty million dollars' worth of gold bars and coins from various nations."

"Holy hell. That's so much better than I expected." Gage tapped a pen on his pad. "All the pieces of the puzzle are coming together. Did the records you found list any medals McKenzie was awarded?"

"Yes, it mentions a good conduct medal, one for overseas service, the soldier's medal, which was awarded for acts of heroism not involving conflict with the enemy and the war medal, which was specific to the Second World War."

"Excellent," Gage said, "that matches my identification of the medals from the tin. Except one." He pushed it toward Sancha. "This one seems to be an oddity. I can't find anything like it in records of war medals from any of the Allied nations. I checked out German medals too in case it was a souvenir he picked up somewhere.

The shape of the cross strikes me as Celtic. It's some kind of yellow metal, and I'd guess the stones are red glass or semi-precious gems."

"Well, it'll have to wait till later. Landry will be happy with what we've found so far. You can start searching images later tonight. We need to do some of the work we're actually paid for."

"You're right." Gage slid the medals into his desk drawer. "What's our next step with our money launderers?"

"I'm always right. What kind of mood are you in?"

"That sounds like a dangerous question," Gage said, suspicious of Sancha's motives.

"Perhaps I should have started with the fact that I know you got laid last night. I guess it involved all kinds of kinky shit, so you should be happy."

"Where is this going, Sancha? You're starting to scare me."

Sancha leaned back in her chair and pressed her fingers together. "Okay, bear with me because I know how you feel about women's intuition but I have a theory."

"Go for it. It's not like we have much else to go on at the moment. A bit of female fulminating can't do any harm."

"Thanks for that resounding vote of confidence and 'female fulminating' — where the hell did that come from?"

"Landry said his mom does it all the time when she's made a decision already but wants his pop to think he had something to do with it." Gage put on his serious face. "You know I have every confidence in you. Now spill it, it's not like you to be reticent."

"This is a bit out there, but what if the money laundering was a front for a diamond heist?"

Gage had enough sense of self-preservation not to laugh. He let Sancha's words roll around his mind, mulling over the theory. "Actually, that's not such a ridiculous idea," he said. "A crime to cover a crime. Set up as a money launderer, build some trust and wait for the big score in the form of a sizable package of gems. That would mean that the guys that stole from Petey, either worked for or were paid by the gem dealer."

"I'd guess worked for. Who else would know about that delivery arriving at a specific time? There's no way it could have been opportunist. That place is buried down a back street. One package was stolen. How could anyone else know the value of an individual package unless they had inside information?"

"So, we were assuming that the firm cleared out because they were afraid of whoever owned the diamonds coming after them because they'd been stolen. That still applies but it must have been planned. If they knew when the robbery was going to happen, they knew they'd have to be gone. I'd guess they cleared out long before the day we went to visit, which means that something doesn't add up."

"The maintenance guy!" Gage and Sancha both shouted at once.

"Fuck, I'm dumber than a box of rocks," Gage said. "I'm gonna be busted down to traffic patrol."

"I'm glad you said I and not we," Sancha said.

"Like I would ever suggest you're as mentally challenged as I clearly am." Gage ran a hand through his hair in frustration. "We need to start running down information on that guy... What was his name?" He leafed through his notebook. "Cyril Kazlo." He slapped the pad against the desk. "Fuck it!"

"Don't beat yourself up, Gage. I spent more time with him than you did. If he was faking it, he was good."

"Hindsight is a wonderful thing. He did know a lot about what went on in that building for someone who was only supposed to be an occasional visitor." Gage sighed. "We need to console ourselves with a big, greasy lunch at the Copper Kettle while we think this over."

"Sounds perfect, let's go." Sancha shoved her chair back. "Maybe one of Pops' triple chocolate milkshakes with whipped cream and sprinkles will reactivate some of your brain cells."

"Fuck!" Gage was disgusted with himself. His shouting drew quite a few amused stares. "I'm not ready to share this yet," he said, in a much lower voice. "Let's go work at Pops' place. We can have pre-lunch snacks, lunch then post-lunch snacks." He high-fived Sancha, who grinned.

"We're back! Superheroes fighting crime. I'll be Batman, you can be Robin."

"The fuck I will," Gage grouched. "I look much better in black than you do."

"You have a point," Sancha said. "And Robin is much cuter, so okay, you can be the weird bat guy, I'll be the clever, intuitive sidekick."

"Remind me never to have an argument with you about anything." Gage grabbed his jacket and headed for the door.

Within half an hour they were both seated at their favorite booth at the Copper Kettle. Gage's appetizer was an enormous bowl of nachos drenched with cheese, salsa and sour cream. Sancha was tackling her second bowl of Rocky Road ice cream.

"We already had pastries and bagels. How are we still hungry?"

"That was hours ago and don't give me that look," Sancha said. "Dessert is a perfectly legitimate appetizer."

Gage crunched down a loaded nacho. "Who am I to judge? Today calls for comfort food regardless of what that might be." Sancha stole one of his nachos. "That mixture, however, is gross."

"It's brain food."

"It's an abomination. It's the kind of thing Landry would eat."

"He's my soulmate." Sancha kept stealing his nachos then dunking them in her ice cream.

"You're both freaks."

"And that's why you love us." Sancha grinned.

Gage slapped his notebook on the table. "So let's work on the assumption that your intuition is right and the pair of us have been a couple of dumbasses."

"Fair enough." Sancha kept eating.

"One. Petey gets mugged dropping off a parcel to what on the surface seems to be a firm of accountants. It's a ruthless attack because he could have died and for all they knew the people who attacked him shoved him in the dumpster thinking he was dead."

"Pair of assholes, check."

"Point two. The accountant's firm that should have received the parcel was a front for a jewel trading business, which in turn was a front for a money laundering operation."

"Complicated, but feasible."

"Point three. The firm cleared out of the building, on first impressions in a hurry. But, and this is a bit of a stretch, that impression could be deliberate."

"Or" — Sancha waved her spoon at Gage — "and this has been playing on my mind, perhaps it *did* happen in a hurry. So much of a hurry that when we arrived to check out the building, they were still finishing up."

"Which would mean that Cyril Kazlo could have been disposing of evidence."

Gage flicked back through his notes. "I'm gonna ring the management company that Kazlo said he worked for." He spent the next ten minutes on his cell then disconnected. "So the company is real and it does have the maintenance contract for that building but there's no record of a recent call-out. and they weren't due to make a routine visit for another month. They don't have an employee by the name of Kazlo."

"Well, fuck." Sancha scraped the last of the ice cream out of her dish. "We were right there with him. We had him."

"I'd like to give your gut a hug right now," Gage said. "We have solid leads. We can assume that Kazlo is either involved, or the brains behind this operation. We know he has at least two accomplices, the men who attacked Petey. Whether or not others at the jewel trader's were aware of what was going on is open to question. We have to assume they were all in on it. It wasn't a big firm, there weren't many desks on the office floor, but they would have needed to stay beneath the radar if they were laundering money via jewel trading. They were biding their time, waiting for the big score, building trust with their clients. They knew when the package would be arriving. It would have been straightforward to make it look like a robbery and, knowing that we would end up investigating the firm, meant that they would have to clear out. Their clients would write off the loss because it's not like they could report it to us. They might try to go after the supposed robbers, but motorcycle helmets and an untrackable vehicle wouldn't give them much to go on. They would have no way of knowing that the robbery wasn't genuine."

"Thieves stealing from thieves. You realize, we're not gonna have much chance of tracking down those muggers either."

"How about I try some theorizing?" Gage said, frowning. "What if those guys never actually took the package with them? What if they handed it over at the time for a quick pay-off?"

Sancha gave a slow nod. "That's entirely possible, but you know what that means?"

Gage shoved his seat back. "We got to that building much quicker than we should have. Kazlo was still there, which means that the jewels may also still be there."

"And he'll have to go back to get them."

"We have to go."

"Yes, yes, we do."

Gage slammed a couple of bills on the table. "Sorry, Pops... We gotta run." Fueled by adrenaline and nachos, he and Sancha raced for the car.

Chapter Fifteen

Landry wriggled and squirmed until he managed to get into his favorite pair of leather pants. It took a liberal application of talcum powder and rigorous calisthenics to get them done up. They even had side zippers at the ankles, they were that tight. He lay on his back with his legs in the air so that he could reach the zippers then flopped flat, panting. "Dressing should not be this difficult. Gage better be grateful...and appreciative." He slithered off the bed then did a bit of rapid crotch adjustment to get comfortable. There was no room for underwear beneath the leather and his bits were complaining about the restriction. He grabbed a T-shirt, not caring which one because he fully intended to remove it later. He and Gage had agreed on a pizza night so he didn't have to worry about cooking. After a long day in the store, he intended to chill on the couch in front of a bad movie until Gage got home. Something involving the imminent destruction of LA or New York would be followed by pizza, mutual consumption of garlicky dough balls and a shared bowl of indulgent tiramisu topped off with a night of kinky sex. The latter being pretty much guaranteed by Landry's pants.

He bopped around the apartment clearing up a bit and was about to pick out a DVD from Gage's growing collection of blow 'em up and disaster movies, when his cell rang. He grabbed it to find a text from Gage saying that he was going to be working late. Landry sighed. "Second place to the Seattle police department," he moaned, but sent a heart emoji back to Gage to let him know that it was no problem. The last thing Gage needed if he was working on an operation was to be worrying that Landry was upset, even if he was feeling a bit sulky. He understood that Gage had an unpredictable job, but his absence was accompanied by an undercurrent of anxiety whenever he wasn't in Landry's line of sight. Landry chuckled. *Gage's possessiveness is rubbing off on me.*

There was no point in staying dressed up for an evening flying solo on the couch. Landry returned to the bedroom, peeled off his pants and dressed instead in a fluffy unicorn onesie that had been a gag gift from Petey. He stole a pair of Gage's thermal socks, the ones he wore when he was going on planned stakeouts, then grabbed his laptop to set up on the dining table. Watching a film no longer held any appeal so Landry decided to get back to his treasure hunting research. Once he was settled with a giant mug of hot chocolate, complete with half a packet of marshmallows, he had a quick flick through his emails. There was one from Sancha outlining a few bullet points about the medals with a note to say that they hadn't had time to investigate the odd one out.

"As good a place to start as any, then." Landry pulled up the picture he had taken of the medals on his phone then began searching through symbols with a similar shape. The starburst shape was unusual, as were the red stones. The medal was very different to most other designs, but it didn't take long before he found a close match. The symbol seemed to be attributed to St. Cuthbert. He found an article about an exhibition of treasure related to the saint at Durham Cathedral in the north of England.

The prize exhibit was a gold and garnet cross that took him down a bit of an Internet rabbit hole. Cuthbert was originally a Celtic Christian and the Celtic connection, plus its shape gave the cross the alternative name Thor's cross.

Landry read a few lines out loud. "Cuthbert means brilliant light. One night in August, 651, the shepherd boy Cuthbert was praying on a hillside near Melrose Monastery which lies at the heart of the Scottish borders. He saw a great light and a choir of angels descend from the night sky.

"The next day he learned that St. Aidan, Bishop of Lindisfarne, had died the previous night. Cuthbert believed he had witnessed St. Aidan's soul being carried to heaven and took this as a sign of his calling to missionary work. Wow. The St. Cuthbert's cross is seen mainly on heraldic regalia and similar ceremonial wear. To fit the shape of escutcheons — I have no idea how to pronounce that — in coats of arms, the cross is formed of four equal length arms. Each arm has a Thor-like hammerhead but there's no connection between Thor and St. Cuthbert except for the influence of Celtic art in the seventh century.

"That's kind of disappointing, a link with Thor would have given me an excuse to look at pictures of blond hunks." He did that anyway, as a reward for his dedication because shirtless pictures of Chris Hemsworth were motivational.

He had to force himself back on topic. He kept reading for a while and various articles all told him much the same. He massaged his temples. He was missing something, he knew it. He was sure he had heard reference to St. Cuthbert somewhere else, but he couldn't recall where. He started revisiting some of the pages that he and Gage had viewed together when they had initially looked up places linked to the treasure map.

An hour later he was cursing his poor memory. He could have saved a lot of time if he'd only remembered that Bellingham in Northumberland, England had a church called St. Cuthbert's.

"Dammit!" He read everything he could find about the church, parts of which dated back to the thirteenth century. He discovered that during building works in 1861, three cannonballs were recovered from within the roof, probably dating from 1597 when Bellingham was attacked by Walter Scott, fifth earl of Buccleuch. That made Landry giggle. "So they weren't so good at cleaning up the stray armaments." Every article he read made reference to St. Cuthbert's well, located adjacent to the church and said to have been discovered by the saint. Supposed to have healing powers, the water was used by the church for baptisms.

"Oh my God! The well." Landry shuffled through the treasure tin and pulled out the book of nursery rhymes. "Ding dong bell, pussy's in the well. I feel sorry for the cat but that has to be it. The treasure never made it to the States, it's in a well in England and I'm the only one that knows it."

Landry wasn't sure whether exhilaration or fear was top of his emotional league table. He'd certainly made it through the play-offs to the Super Bowl. He got up then went to check the lock on the apartment door. "Gage is rubbing off on me," he muttered. He checked the time and was shocked that it was almost two in the morning. The Internet had sucked him into a wormhole. He shivered, despite his cozy outfit. His jubilation at putting the pieces of the puzzle trail together was diminished by worry over Gage's whereabouts.

Landry busied himself in the bathroom for a while then climbed into a bed that was far too cold. He snuggled beneath the comforter, cuddling Gage's pillow. There was no way he was going to sleep, there was far too much rattling around in his head. He was desperate to talk to Gage but knew better than to call or message him. If he was in a position where a ring tone or message alert betrayed him, Landry would never forgive himself, and Gage couldn't be relied on to silence his phone.

Landry dozed but he couldn't sleep. He was excited about the possibility that he might have solved one of the greatest mysteries of modern times, frustrated that in the middle of the night he had no one to tell, and terrified that whoever else sought the treasure would come after him again. He wasn't convinced that his fake map would keep them off the scent for long. On top of all that, he was worried about Gage and what had happened during the day to keep him away so long. He thumped Gage's pillow. "You are not supposed to scare me like this. You're supposed to take care of me always." He was exhausted, stressed and he needed his Dom's arms around him. The moment he caught the scrape of a key in the front door he became more alert. Other than Gage, only Petey had a key and he would have texted or called first. Landry still grabbed the nearest thing to hand as a weapon.

"Why are you waving my best paddle at me?" Gage loomed in the bedroom doorway, his smirk clear even in the low light. Landry turned on a lamp.

"Where have you been? Are you okay?" He dropped the paddle.

"We cracked the money laundering case. Caught the bad guys. It got a bit rough but an hour ago I had a million plus dollars' worth of uncut diamonds in my hands." Landry was out of bed and across the room in an instant. "What in the ever-loving heck are you wearing?" Gage pushed back the hood of Landry's unicorn onesie.

"It's your fault. I was wearing skin-tight leather until you told me you weren't coming back. I had to get comfy." Landry started stripping Gage where he stood. "Tell me about the diamonds!"

"What are you doing?"

"I need to check you over. Do I need to fetch the first aid kit?"

Gage stood passive while Landry removed all his clothes. "It's the middle of the night and I'm standing here, butt ass naked in the company of a furry unicorn. I think I may have been shot and this is some kind of hallucination brought on by seriously good drugs."

"Hush, you. Oh my God, your shoulder is some kind of bruisy rainbow."

"That's what happens when you have to barge down a door because the police department are busy using their battering ram elsewhere."

"Why did *you* have to do it?"

"It was me or Sancha."

"Fair enough," Landry grumbled. "Though, I bet Sancha has really hard shoulders." He kept prodding and poking. "Your hip is bruised too."

"I hit the ground when I went through the door. Had to dive in case anyone was shooting at me."

"And were they?" Landry had to ask.

"If they were, they didn't hit me and that's all you need to know." A very naked Gage drew Landry into his arms. "I'm fine. A bit battered that's all. It was a great result and the best thing of all is that Petey can relax. No one's going to be coming after him now."

"That's amazing news. Give me the highlights."

"To cut a long story short, we realized that the money laundering was a cover-up for a jewel theft from some unsavory people and that we'd interrupted their getaway plan. A fake maintenance guy had hidden the diamonds in the plumbing, and they weren't found when the building was searched. We worked out that he'd have to go back to get them, lay in wait and bingo. Bad guy caught, diamonds retrieved, case closed."

"That's amazing! I had an exciting evening too," Landry said as Gage hoisted him into his arms, two hands beneath his butt. He walked him back to the bed then dropped him onto the mattress.

"You can tell me all about it once we're warm." Gage got into bed too and pulled the comforter over the pair of them.

"I've solved the riddle of the map," Landry said. He gave Gage a very brief summary of how all the clues had slotted together.

"If this turns out to be right, it's quite a story." Gage pulled Landry closer. "But as we have to be up again in about three hours, we need to try and grab at least a little sleep otherwise we're both going to feel like hell in the morning."

"I think that's a given," Landry said. "I'm going to be mainlining coffee for the entire day. I can sleep now you're here. I was scared."

"I'm sorry I worried you," Gage murmured, stroking Landry's hair. "Everything happened real fast. When Sancha gets one of her gut feelings, she really knows how to put a bee up the collective backside of the Seattle PD."

"Bees and backsides do not go together," Landry muttered, closing his eyes. Gage's warmth and scent surrounded him and finally he could relax.

He slept for ten minutes — at least that was what it felt like to Landry when he awoke, groggy, bleary-eyed and cranky. Gage was already up, hair damp from the shower and half-dressed. Landry summoned the energy to ogle his bare chest before he buttoned his shirt. "I wish I had the strength to come over there and lick you."

"Coffee is brewing. Once Sancha and I are done questioning the guys we took in last night, I mean this morning... I have no idea what the time is, I should be able to finish early."

"Sounds good." Landry stretched, groaning at his aching joints. "I foresee an early night in our future. How long has it been since we got eight solid hours of sleep?"

"Too long. And right now just thinking about it makes me want to yawn."

"No! Don't do that or you'll set me off." Landry hid beneath the duvet, but Gage peeled it back to give him a kiss.

"Go take a cold shower, that'll help."

"Sadist."

"Occasionally." Gage grinned. "I'll see you soon. Be good."

"I'm always good!" Landry yelled after him before subsiding back under the covers. "Ten more minutes…"

Despite his words and his body's need for rest, Landry rolled out of bed a few minutes later then dragged himself to the shower. He didn't resort to cold water because he wasn't a masochist but he did have it cooler than normal. He got dry, drank coffee, dressed, drank more coffee then stumbled down the stairs about fifteen minutes later than he should have.

"You look like a pile of steaming dog crap," Petey said.

"And there's my supportive best friend at work," Landry grumbled.

"I hope those suitcases under your eyes are Louis Vuitton and that they were worth it."

"I'll tell you all about it once I've been to the café for vast quantities of sugar-laden baked goodies and a couple gallons of coffee. You want anything?"

Petey rolled his eyes. "You really are half-asleep if you have to ask me that."

"I'm a lost cause. Thanks for opening up, oh and Gage solved his case, so you don't have a target painted on your ass anymore!"

"Really? Oh, wow that's fabulous. You can tell me about it when you get back. Go!" Petey shooed him toward the door. "If the customers catch sight of you, they'll run away."

Landry stuck his tongue out at his friend then held the door open for an incoming customer. He slipped around the man, noting his Seahawks baseball cap with a wry grin. If the guy wanted to start up a conversation about sports with Petey he'd be seriously out of luck. Petey had trouble telling the difference between a baseball and a football.

Landry stood on the sidewalk and raised his face to the sun. For once it was warm and bright. He took a deep breath, taking in the familiar, mingled scents of coffee and baking from the café, incense from the Eastern Emporium across the street, and the unique smell of slowly warming asphalt. On the roofline opposite, two fat pigeons sat, eyeing him. He gave them a little wave. "No crumbs for you yet, girls."

As he reached the café door, his cell rang. Sighing, he pulled it from his pocket and moved away from the door. There was a line, and he didn't want to stand there airing his business to assorted coffee addicts awaiting their morning fix. They'd be grumpy enough as it was. He glanced at the number, but it was withheld. Shrugging, he connected the call assuming that it was most likely someone trying to sell him insurance or telling him that the FBI was about to arrest him because of all the porn in his browsing history.

"Hello."

"How wonderful to hear your dulcet tones, Landry."

Landry fumbled the phone from one ear to the other, not sure he was hearing correctly. "Is that you, James?"

"And there I was thinking I was the only Englishman you were intimately acquainted with. I'll be bitterly disappointed if you tell me you've been consorting with my countrymen behind my back."

"The only consorting I do is with Gage."

"The annoying detective is still keeping you captive, is he?"

"I'm not discussing my sex life with you. How did you get this number, anyway? Where are you?" Landry looked around, half-expecting Ellery to appear from behind a streetlight.

"I'm an investigator, Landry. Give me a little credit for being able to get my hands on information I require and I'm in London, so you can stop trying to spot me."

"That's a relief, and you're a thief. Having a plummy accent doesn't change that."

"I say tomatoes, you say tomaytoes. And who pronounces it that way? If I had time to get into a conversation with you right now about your pronunciation issues, I would but I don't."

"Well, if you're in such a rush, tell me what you want." Landry leaned against the nearest wall. "I haven't had nearly enough coffee yet this morning. I was about to go into the bakery, so this conversation is keeping me away from sugar and carbs. You're on dangerous ground, believe me."

"I apologize for interrupting your morning. I recommend a nice cup of English breakfast tea, and a toasted muffin with Marmite."

"We are not having this conversation. Get to the point, James, or I'm hanging up."

"I wouldn't do that if I were you. I want you to walk back to Treasure Trove and take a look through the window."

With a pained sigh, Landry wandered back to the store. Inside he could see Petey was still dealing with the customer in the baseball cap. "I'm here. What am I supposed to be looking at?"

"You should be looking at a friend of mine. A football fan. And I'm talking about your strange concept of football not the beautiful game. You and I are going to have a nice friendly chat and if you're cooperative, my friend will not pull out the rather unpleasant, serrated knife he keeps beneath his coat and apply it to your young friend's skin."

At that moment, the man in the baseball cap turned and looked directly at Landry. He winked before turning back to Petey and engaging in conversation.

"This is turning into a seriously shitty morning." Landry stomped along the street a way then took a seat on the low wall outside St. Peters, praying that there weren't too many creepy crawlies inhabiting the moss-covered stones. "What the hell, James? Threatening my friends is not nice."

"Now, now. You need to be a good boy."

"I am so far from being your boy..." Landry glanced heavenward, scowling. "What do you want to talk about, as if I didn't know?"

"So you worked out it was me that sent you the map?"

"You sent me the postcard warning me to hide it, didn't you?"

"I did. The map's existence became a little too public, and I was concerned that competitors of mine might track it to you."

"They did, you son of a bitch. They attacked Gage, got into my apartment... They are not nice people."

"But you didn't give it to them, did you?" For the first time, Landry thought he detected a trace of uncertainty in James Ellery's voice.

"Gage is fine, thanks for asking. They think they have it. They don't."

"Excellent, and, for what it's worth, I'm glad your detective wasn't damaged. I assume you have followed the clues?"

"I'm guessing that you know I have, or you wouldn't be calling," Landry said.

"You guess correctly. Very insightful. My spies tell me you've been a very busy boy. I hope your trip to Bellingham was fruitful. Unfortunately, my past activities prevent me from visiting the United States at the moment, so I needed someone to carry out some investigations on my behalf. I knew I could rely on your inquisitive mind to be intrigued enough by a treasure map to follow up the clues. You spotted the watermark."

"Yes," Landry said. "Was it real?"

"I can assure you the map is genuine. I came across it quite by accident. It was hidden inside a book that was part of a lot of items I picked up at an estate sale at a stately home in Northumberland. The place had housed a group of American servicemen being sent back to the States. When they left, they had to travel light so heavy things like books were left behind. The map dropped a lot of hints but nothing substantial enough to give me a location for the portrait."

"It *is* the Rafael painting at the end of this wild goose chase, then?" Landry asked.

"Oh yes. It's just unfortunate that the thief concerned transported it back to the United States. I have a grudging respect for his ingenuity. It must have been quite a task to keep it hidden." Landry didn't say a word. "There's something you're not telling me, Landry my sweet. It's in the best interest of you and your friend not to hold anything back."

"First of all, I want you to tell me a few things."

"You're hardly in a position to negotiate but I like you, so ask away." There was a clink of teacups in the background.

"Having a tea break?" Landry asked. "What time is it over there, anyway?"

"It's late afternoon. The perfect time for a cup of reviving Earl Grey. Not that there isn't a good time for tea, obviously."

"Obviously."

"What do you want to know, Landry? I'm feeling magnanimous due to the ready supply of chocolate Hobnobs on a plate not very far from me."

"First, why didn't you just send me the map instead of going through the whole charade with the leaflet, the antiques fair, the gilded mirror... You couldn't possibly have known that everything would go to plan."

"I needed you to think, at least initially, that you had come across the map by accident. It wasn't that difficult to entice you along to the fair, though I confess to being somewhat shocked that Detective Roskam goes through his in-tray on a regular basis. It was a simple matter to send a bunch of flyers into his precinct for distribution."

"The stallholder, was he in on this?"

"He was tasked with getting the mirror to you. He didn't know what it contained. He's one of Tad's many uncles. If he'd missed you at the fair, he would have brought the mirror into Treasure Trove and offered it to you at a ridiculous price. Even if you hadn't bought it for yourself, you would have been obliged to dismantle it to check it over for restoration but as it was, extending the subterfuge wasn't necessary. I did tell him that you were passionate about lucky cats and to make sure he had something on the stall that would draw your eye."

"You are one manipulative, sneaky son of a bitch."

"Why, thank you. That's quite the compliment."

"It wasn't meant to be," Landry grumbled. "So why the warning postcard? That's what gave it away that you had to be involved."

"You were meant to be my tool. This little adventure wasn't supposed to put you in danger, that wasn't my intent, but I became aware of other…interested parties. I needed investment from my company and somehow, news of the map leaked to a competitor. These people are not known for their benevolence when it comes to hunting down rare objects."

"I put them off the scent," Landry said. "But they might come back. If I get hurt because of your plotting, Gage will hunt you down and remove parts of your anatomy, you know that."

"I knew you would be resourceful. When the portrait is revealed, they'll no longer have any need to come after you, and Gage will have no need to subject British customs to what I know must be a terrifying passport photograph. Another reason, if you need one, to point me at its location, wouldn't you say?"

Landry sighed again—James Ellery had that effect on him. His mind was working overtime. He couldn't get to England to look for the painting himself. His only course of action would be to contact the authorities in the UK who would probably laugh at him and that wouldn't do anything to help Petey, who was stuck inside Treasure Trove with a psycho.

"I can hear the cogs in your brain whirring from over here," James said. "I'm sure you've realized by now that the only sensible course of action is to tell me what you found over there and where I need to go to retrieve the pretty young man."

"I still don't quite understand," Landry said. "You won't be able to keep the portrait and there can't be any insurance value attached to it, so what's in it for you?"

"I'd have thought that would be obvious," James said. "It would of course seal my reputation as the foremost treasure hunter of my generation. Handing it over will give both my company and myself a huge amount of positive publicity. We will have business coming out of our ears and my current difficulties with international travel will be resolved. The authorities tend to be grateful when treasures of such historical importance are retrieved."

Landry rolled his shoulders in an attempt to ease some of the tension in his joints. "I should have known that philanthropy wasn't your first objective."

"I think there's been enough dissection of my character for now. We can resume this conversation when I'm able to come and visit you in person once again. But for now, it's time for you to tell me what I need to know because believe me, Landry, it would be the work of a moment to contact my colleague and get him to put a few superfluous holes into your friend's body. I do so appreciate text technology."

"I really don't like you," Landry said. "Gage is gonna use you for target practice if you ever set foot back on US soil, and I'm gonna watch."

"Detective Roskam and I have a special relationship," James said. "A bit like the UK and America. Now tell me what I need to know, Landry. It's distasteful to have to make threats."

Landry huffed and gave James a potted summary of all the clues he'd worked out and how they fitted together. "So you see, he never did bring the painting back here."

"I do see. The man must have gained a conscience at some point. If the painting is still where you believe it to be, I hope that he protected it well."

"Will you go and look for it?"

"Of course. I'm hardly going to sit here in London when it could be just a few hours away. Knowing that it's here in England makes my life a great deal easier."

Landry walked back to stand in front of Treasure Trove. "I've given you what you wanted, you asshole. Now get your thug out of my store." The call disconnected. Landry wanted to scream into his cell but settled for stamping his foot. "That man makes me want to get stabby!"

There was a jingle as the bell above Treasure Trove's front door rang and the man in the baseball cap walked out, clutching a brown paper-wrapped parcel. He nodded at Landry then strolled off down the street as if he were out and about on any shopping trip. Landry ran into the store and went straight up to Petey. He checked him over. "Phew, no additional holes."

"What are you talking about?" Petey pushed him away. "And where's my hot chocolate and cake? You've been gone ages. Did you get distracted by a squirrel again?"

"That guy you were just with, did he hurt you?"

"I have no idea what you're talking about Landry, have you been taking something? I just made a great sale. He bought a load of sports memorabilia, some old baseball programs and that signed football that's been moldering in the corner for months."

Landry stared at him. "He didn't...do anything?"

"Other than pay me a great deal of money, no." Petey pressed the backs of his fingers to Landry's forehead. "Are you feeling all right? He said a friend in the UK had recommended the store and told him to visit. He was glad he did—texted his pal to let him know he was here and everything."

"That no good, lying, smarmy, too-handsome-for-his-own-good, fucking Brit!" Landry's cell dinged to advise him of an incoming text. He opened it to find a single emoji of a winking face. "Fuck me sideways." Landry slumped into the leather club chair with a groan. "Take a seat, honey. I have a lot to tell you. This is gonna take a while. It's the story of how your best friend in the world thought he was saving your behind when he was actually being taken for a ride by a criminal mastermind."

"Sounds exciting." Petey dropped into the nearest chair.

"Not exactly what I'd call it, but here goes."

Chapter Sixteen

When Gage, true to his promise, showed up at Treasure Trove shortly after lunchtime he had Mr. Lao in tow. Landry, who had been hiding in the stock cupboard, peeked around the doorway.

"How does he look?" he stage whispered to Petey who was standing with his back to the door.

"Hot, in that dark, broody way he has going on, and, by the way, he either knows you're behind me or thinks I have a serious problem with talking to myself."

"I thought we discussed you using your ventriloquist voice," Landry hissed.

"And I told you I don't have one. The closest I come to talking with my mouth closed is when Carter brings out his gag collection."

"Way too much information, Petey."

"Why are you hiding from Gage anyway?"

"Because as soon as he sees me he is gonna know I've been talking to James Ellery and he's not gonna like it. I like fun spankings, not punishment paddlings."

"You're going to have to tell him everything anyway. It looks like he's brought Mr. Lao back with him so the two of you can spend some quality time together."

"Any other day that would make me all kinds of happy," Landry said. "He's right there, isn't he?"

"Uh huh."

"The only reason for you to be hiding in that cupboard, Landry Carran, is because you have a guilty conscience."

Landry swore the deep timbre of Gage's voice vibrated through his bones.

"Did you break something, Landry?" Mr. Lao had trust issues.

Landry sidled out from his hiding place to stand behind the cash desk. "Of course I didn't break anything Mr. L. When did I ever...? No, don't answer that. Your stock is safe, and we've had a great day for sales so far, though I have to admit Petey's done most of the work." Petey preened a little when Mr. Lao gave him a pat on the head.

"You're a good boy, Petey. You and I will have a fun afternoon while Gage and Landry catch up on some much-needed sleep. The pair of you look like you've been burning the candle at both ends using a flamethrower rather than a match."

Gage chuckled. "We're going to take a walk first, get some fresh air and a hot dog with all the trimmings. Landry is going to tell me what he's been up to then we are going to come back here and sleep for at least twelve hours."

Petey snickered but soon stopped between Gage's stare and the clip round the ear Mr. Lao gave him. "What did I do?"

"It's what you were thinking, not doing," Mr. Lao said with a knowing smile.

"I can see everything is well under control here." Gage smirked. "Grab your jacket, Landry. Let's go."

Landry made sure he had his wallet, keys and cell before trailing Gage down the center aisle of the store to the door. He gave Petey and Mr. Lao a small wave before Gage, with an impatient huff, grabbed his wrist and towed him out onto the sidewalk.

"Food before confessions. I've been craving a hotdog all morning."

Landry nibbled on his lower lip then turned his attention to his thumbnail.

"It wasn't my fault."

"I'm sure it wasn't," Gage said. "Whatever *it* was."

"Just trying for some pre-emptive self-defense," Landry said. "Before you start using your good cop, bad cop interrogation techniques on me."

"You and I both know, Landry that you're gonna fold like a pack of cards the minute I scowl at you. You've not been able to hide anything from me since the moment we met. You couldn't lie if the fate of the entire planet depended on it."

Landry didn't bother to deny it because it was true. If he attempted so much as a minor fib, his face glowed the color of a British telephone box.

"Why do they paint stuff red anyway? Buses, mailboxes, those old-fashioned telephone kiosks… It's all red. P'raps their government has shares in red paint."

"Would I be right in assuming that someone has got you thinking about the British?" Gage slipped his sunglasses from his jacket pocket then put them on. He turned his mirrored gaze onto Landry. "Because that sentence came out of nowhere."

Landry was torn between annoyance at not being able to read Gage's expression and satisfaction at how hot his boyfriend looked in a pair of aviators. "If I say yes, I'm going to incriminate myself, aren't I?"

"You're way beyond that, sweetheart, believe me."

"There's a reason Brits always play bad guys in the movies, you know." Landry dragged his feet all the way to the hotdog cart at the edge of the small neighborhood park a few blocks from Treasure Trove but then perked up at the scent of frying onions. His stomach rumbled. "I want the works on mine," he said, then added, "and a double portion of onions."

"Make that two." Gage placed the order. "You want a soda?"

"I'll take a water, please." Landry didn't want to add bubbles to his already unsettled stomach. They took their food to a nearby bench, and Landry planted his ass on the unyielding wood.

"He texted me," Gage said, managing to sound both annoyed and resigned.

"Who?" Landry said around a mouthful of unidentifiable meat product.

"Don't try that with me, Landry." Gage used his thumb to wipe a smear of mustard from the corner of Landry's mouth before pulling out his cell and displaying a text that consisted of a single winking emoji.

"You're talking about James Ellery. Are the two of you having some kind of bromance I should know about? Why does he have your number?"

Gage chewed, swallowed then looked Landry directly in the eye. "I am not averse to the idea of bending you over the back of this bench and giving you a sound thrashing. My number isn't a secret. He texted to let me know that you and he had engaged in a mutually satisfying exchange earlier today."

Landry fidgeted. "It might have been satisfying for him! Yes, James called me. He was working with a guy who came into the store when I went out for coffee. He said this guy would hurt Petey if I didn't tell him, James that is, everything about solving the clues from the treasure map. So I did. He's probably already on his way to the well in Bellingham."

"Good."

"What do you mean good? He said that Petey would get stabbed if I didn't tell him everything. How is that good?"

"Petey is fine, isn't he? There was never any danger."

"How do you know that?"

"Because it's not Ellery's style. He's manipulative and ruthless but I don't believe he'd ever actually hurt anyone to get his way. He doesn't need to."

"It seemed pretty real to me," Landry muttered. "But his accomplice, whoever he was, winked at me when he left the store and he bought loads of stuff. Petey was over the moon with the sale he made, and he had no idea what was going on."

"Ellery probably just asked the guy to go into the store if he saw you leave. Told him to hang around near the cash desk. It would only have taken a quick text from him to let Ellery know that things were in place."

"I'm so dumb." Landry leaned against Gage's solid form. "I should have known he was lying."

"No you're not. You thought you were protecting your friend. You did exactly the right thing."

"But he'll find the treasure."

"Actually, he won't."

"Why do you sound so smug?" Landry rubbed his cheek against Gage's stubble.

"Because I haven't been sitting around eating donuts, despite what you think I do all day. I emailed a contact in the UK. Told him he needed to go well diving in Northumberland and that he ought to hang around and see who showed up."

"You did? Why didn't you tell me?"

"Because I had a very strong feeling that Mr. Ellery would get in touch with you sooner or later. He set all this up. He put us on the trail. One way or another he would have had to have gotten the information out of you and I guess he has some serious competition. I'd place money that the men we saw near the waterfall are his rivals."

"So you set a trap?" Landry nuzzled into the crook of Gage's neck. "You're as devious as he is. Why does that turn me on when it's you but when it's him it makes my flesh crawl?"

Gage walked his fingers up Landry's thigh. "Because you are a kinky, kinky boy and that's why I love you."

"So what happens next?" Landry balled up the wrapper from his dog. "Will your contact in the UK let you know what's going on?"

"As soon as he can, he will. It might be a while, and we promised ourselves a bit of hibernation time, didn't we?"

Landry took a swig from his bottle of water. "I am badly in need of recuperation. I had a very stressful morning."

"And that's why Mr. Lao will be keeping Petey company for the rest of the day while you and I are horizontal and unconscious."

"Sounds dreamy."

Gage yawned. "I could sleep for a week. Solving a big case is great but the paperwork afterward is enough to try the patience of a saint. You know, diamonds in the rough look like rocks. Nothing special at all. I guess I thought they'd be more exciting."

"You and Sancha have been on a treasure hunt too, even though you didn't realize it. I need sleep but we can fit in some awake stuff as well, can't we?" Landry attempted his most appealing look making big eyes and pouty lips.

"It's always good to test the limits of our endurance," Gage said, grabbing Landry's hand. He took their litter and lobbed it into the nearest trash can with perfect aim. "How long were you going to wait before you told me about Ellery's call?"

"As soon as I saw you," Landry said. "Promise."

"In that case, I'll go easy on the spanking." Gage gave Landry's butt a pat. "I have plans for that paddle you were waving at me last night. You know, you looked more like you were trying to bring a plane into land than defend yourself."

"Hey! It was the first thing I got hold of. It's not like we keep a baseball bat under the bed and besides, the only ball sports I was ever any good at didn't involve a bat. Can we go back through the store? I want you to reassure Petey that the money laundering case is done and dusted. I told him all about it, but he'll be more relaxed if he hears it from you."

"Okay. I told Carson everything as well. Petey has nothing to worry about. The men that attacked him were hired to steal the package, nothing more. Petey was collateral damage."

They ambled the few blocks back but as they reached the store, the sound of shattering glass greeted them.

"Are you sure about that?" Landry ran for the door only for Gage to catch him around the waist and lift him out of the way.

"You stay right here. Call 911, then call Sancha but do not come into the store. Do you understand me? This is not negotiable." Gage drew his gun. "Do it, Landry. Then get away from here. Got to the café." Landry nodded, trying not to panic. He pulled out his cell and got dialing as Gage shouldered his way through the door.

Having decided that, in this case, attack was the best form of defense, Gage slammed his way into Treasure Trove. The door had been latched, but it gave way with a crack of splintering wood. Pain lanced through Gage's already injured shoulder, but he gritted his teeth and ignored it. With a speed born of experience, he assessed the situation even as he weaved down the central aisle of the store toward the cash desk at the rear. Underfoot, broken glass and china crunched at every step. "Seattle PD, armed police, drop your weapons!"

A blur of bodies was engaged in a full-on fight behind the cash desk and nobody took a blind bit of notice of him. Gage caught sight of Petey on all fours, half-hidden behind a wooden trunk. Except he wasn't hiding. He was whacking at the legs of two men with what looked like an antique carpet beater. The two strangers in the store bore a remarkable resemblance to the men that had tracked Gage and Landry on the waterfall hike, the same men that had taken the map, though they weren't now wearing balaclavas. Gage ducked as a gun, knocked from someone's hand, flew overhead. Keeping low, he scuttled forward.

One of the men landed at his feet with a thud and he wasted no time in rolling him onto his front then cuffing him. The man didn't resist, seeming dazed. Blood trickled from his nose. Pushing his prone form to one side, Gage got cautiously to his feet. Mr. Lao was busy channeling his inner Jet Li, delivering a sound thrashing to the other man who still had a grip on his gun but had absolutely no chance of using it.

Gage looked on, impressed as Mr. Lao delivered a spectacular kick to the man's jaw, bringing him to his knees where Petey bashed him across the back of the head with his carpet beater, laying him out flat. Gage only carried one pair of cuffs, but he did have cable ties in his pocket and used them to incapacitate the second man.

"Thank you for your invaluable help, Detective Roskam," Mr. Lao said, grinning from ear to ear. He grabbed Petey's hand and pulled him to his feet. "Nicely done, Petey. I think you've proved the usefulness of that carpet beater. Packs quite a wallop, doesn't it?"

Petey, face flushed and hair tousled gave him a high five. "We rock."

"Would one of you'd like to tell me what's going on?" Gage surveyed the damage around him. It seemed to be limited to the immediate area around the cash desk. Petey and Mr. Lao both started talking at once and he had to hush them.

"One of you, please."

"I'll make some green tea, Mr. L, while you talk to Gage," Petey said. "I think we could both do with a cup, don't you?"

"Fine idea. Make a cup for the detective as well, he's looking a little tense."

Gage shook his head. "On second thoughts, I need to let the cavalry know that they don't have to come charging in here, guns blazing. Landry's outside and he must be climbing the walls by now. Give me a minute then you can tell us all at the same time what's been going on." He checked on the two men on the floor. One was moaning while the other was out cold but breathing fine. He nudged the noisy one with the toe of his boot. "Quiet, moron, or I'll give you back to the old guy." The threat worked and the moaning subsided to muttered curses. Gage made it one step outside the door onto the sidewalk before he got an armful of Landry.

"I thought I told you to get away from here." Landry clung to him like a limpet.

"I did. I made the calls like you told me to. I walked at least ten paces down the street, which was really far but then I decided it would be safe to peek through the window, but I couldn't see anything. Is everyone okay in there, Mr. Lao and Petey?"

"They're fine and apparently quite capable of looking after themselves. You can come in but be careful where you walk because there's a lot of broken glass and china on the floor."

"What?" Landry squirmed out of Gage's arms and ran inside.

"I'm kidding myself if I ever thought I'd have any control over that boy," Gage muttered. He was about to follow him inside when two patrol cars screeched up to the curb. Sancha scrambled out of one of them.

"Holy mother, Roskam. If this is your idea of taking the afternoon off to catch up on your sleep…"

"You can't blame me for this, Sancha," Gage protested, glaring at his uniformed colleagues who were all laughing. "There are two criminals inside who need to be taken in, so you lot can deal with that rather than standing around smirking. They may need to see a medic."

"Did you not get enough action last night?" Sancha stood with her hands on her hips, scowling.

"Seriously, it wasn't me. Mr. Lao and Petey took both of them down before I got the chance to get involved."

"You sound so affronted." Sancha bent double, laughing.

"I had to barge through another door. How about some sympathy?" Gage rubbed his sore shoulder, but Sancha got even more hysterical while the patrol officers went into the store to collect the bad guys.

"You are definitely dealing with the paperwork on this one," Sancha said, wiping tears from her eyes.

"I'm off duty," Gage protested. "I need sleep even more now. Fuck me, I'm getting too old for this." He groaned as a fire truck, sirens blaring, pulled up in the middle of the street. Carson and his entire crew spilled out.

"What the actual fuck, Gage?" Carson stomped toward him.

"Nothing's on fire, Carson."

"I don't give a shit. Someone put in a call for paramedics, and where they go we go, so we're here. Now, where's Petey?"

"Inside. He's fine. Shall we all go in. Jesus, I'm getting a migraine."

Everyone trooped into Treasure Trove and the number of people made the store seem cramped and claustrophobic.

"Who wants tea?" Petey shouted above the general hubbub. There was a chorus of requests and a lot of waving hands. Mr. Lao was handing round a plate of cookies while the two sizable uniformed cops were dragging their protesting prisoners toward the door.

Gage took in the scene, mouth open.

"You're going to catch flies in that." Landry gave him a smacking kiss right there in front of everyone. There were cookie crumbs around his mouth. "Mr. Lao's girlfriend made these cookies—they have real stem ginger in them." He thrust one into Gage's hand. "I'll get you a cup of Mr. Lao's disgusting tea. I'm not having one because, bleh, but your stomach's made of cast-iron."

Carson walked over to them, his arm around Petey's shoulders. Petey gave him a shy smile. "Thanks for coming to the rescue, Gage. I was really pleased to see you, even though you did break the door and it's not been that long since it was fixed."

"From what I saw, you didn't need me at all." Gage crunched on his cookie. "This is excellent."

"Well, we didn't have any handcuffs. At least, we didn't have any down here because Carson keeps a few pairs in my apartment, and I'm sure you and Landry have a supply, but I wasn't going to run upstairs for them and leave Mr. Lao on his own. Did you know he's been studying martial arts for over sixty years?"

Gage caught Carson's grin and scowled. "I didn't know that. No one ever thought to mention it." Landry was taking care to look in a different direction. The ninja in question wandered over. "Quite a mess they made. They kept falling into things. Very odd. Still, I have great insurance, and Landry keeps a detailed record of the stock. With a detective as a witness, I should have no trouble with my claim. Petey, you need to clear some of these people out of the store. They are all too big and clumsy. They can drink tea and eat cookies on the street."

Carson grinned then bellowed some orders that had everyone in a uniform trooping out to the sidewalk. Bemused, Gage took in the destruction, the abandoned carpet beater, and the spots of blood on the floor. Sancha took pity on him.

"You and Landry get out of here. I'll take statements from our two superheroes and then follow the arresting officers back to the precinct to interview the wannabe criminals. What a pair of losers."

"The same losers we saw when we were hiking in Bellingham," Gage said, "and probably the ones who attacked me here. I can't be a hundred percent sure, but if you interrogate them about their movements, you might get lucky."

"So this takes us back to Landry's treasure map," Sancha said. "For a single piece of paper, it's managed to cause an awful lot of trouble."

Landry had grabbed a broom and was sweeping glittering shards of glass and broken china into a heap.

"Leave that, Lan. I'll do it," Petey said. "You were looking dead on your feet hours ago. You and Gage really do need to get some sleep."

Landry leaned on the broom. Gage wondered if it was the only thing holding him up. He held out a hand to Landry, who propped his broom against a nearby wardrobe before taking it.

"Sounds like great advice," Landry said, fighting a yawn.

"So now you're learning to take orders," Gage muttered. "I'm going wrong somewhere. You, me, bed."

"Yes, Sir." Landry managed half a smile. "See, I can be obedient."

Spluttering his disbelief, Gage guided him to the door. "Of course you can."

Chapter Seventeen

"This is so unfair!" Landry attempted to hump the pillow Gage had lodged beneath his belly. He was naked, his wrists cuffed behind him, a spreader bar keeping his legs apart. "My ass is in the air, why aren't you taking advantage with that big, fat d—?"

"Landry... That mouth of yours is going to get you into a lot of trouble." Gage planted a couple of hard smacks on Landry's exposed cheeks. "What did I tell you earlier?"

"To be quiet and still. To meditate on my situation." Landry thumped the mattress. "But that was before you got the vibrator out. I don't like my situation! I am not the Dalai Lama—he seems like a cool dude, but even he couldn't meditate in this position."

"Quit whining or I'll gag you." Gage held the offending toy against Landry's balls then turned it on. "We haven't spent nearly as much quality time together recently as we should. You've been taking liberties. You're a brat, a bad influence on Petey, and I feel the need to remind you that you are my submissive. My obedient, compliant, sweet-natured submissive."

Landry snorted. Then regretted it as his balls got another dose of vibration. "Please, Sir. Need you in me."

"That's what you want. I decide what you need, and as Mr. Lao is keeping the store closed today while the door is replaced, I have all the time in the world to make sure those needs are appropriately met."

"Don't you have to work? We slept all yesterday afternoon and all night."

"Nope. Sancha and I both have the day off because we closed the money laundering case. Not that it *was* money laundering in the end but regardless, I have a whole day to torture you."

"Oh goody. But you got to come already. I gave you a world-class blow job, you said so. Then I got you breakfast in bed and I let you share my coffee."

"You had a whole pot." Gage shifted the vibrator from Landry's balls to the sensitive skin around his hole.

"Your point being?"

Gage replaced the vibrator with his tongue and Landry screamed. "Too much! Too good! If I don't come, I'm gonna pop!"

Gage carried on rimming him, probing with his extremely talented tongue, pulling Landry's ass cheeks apart for better access. Landry could no longer form coherent words as a wave of heat swept down his spine and a sheen of perspiration coated his skin. He panted, unable to suck in enough oxygen. His dick was so hard it hurt. He felt loose, ready, but Gage still tormented him, replacing his tongue with one finger, then two and a liberal dose of lube. Landry had a fleeting thought that he might require the services of a brown paper bag if he got any closer to hyperventilating, but the thought dissolved into vapor as Gage thrust into him.

"Are your shoulders okay?" Maddeningly, Gage stilled.

"Gage…"

"You've been in cuffs a while, so tell me you're okay or I stop."

"Every single part of my very cute anatomy is absolutely perfect," Landry hissed. "But various bits of me are going to die of frustration really, really soon. They're going to curl up and die. Is that what you want?" He jiggled his wrists in an attempt to demonstrate just how okay he was. Jiggling his ass came next and that drew a curse from Gage who finally, finally began to move. Landry sent a silent prayer of gratitude heavenward.

Apparently inspired by divine intervention, Gage proceeded to pound Landry into the mattress. Landry squealed his delight and went with the bouncing, quite happy for Gage to take full control. Gage grunted with every thrust, punctuating his efforts with a few well-chosen words.

"Fuck. You're. Tight."

Landry grinned, as much as he was able when his face was being rubbed against the bed sheets. He loved being the cause of Gage's inability to communicate with more than one word at a time. Landry couldn't reach for his dick but came regardless and as soon as he started Gage reached around his body to give him a helping hand. He may have screamed, he wasn't sure, but the moment was worthy of vocal proclamation. To Landry's delight, the normally stoic Gage was in accord and yelled as he came, his body shaking as his second orgasm of the morning rolled through him. Emotion overwhelmed Landry and he sobbed his joy, dampening the sheets with his tears. For a long while, Gage held still, sucking in deep breaths, gripping Landry's hips as if preventing his escape. Landry had no intention of going anywhere. His sobs turned to giggles.

"That was phantasmagorical!" His body shook with laughter.

"I don't even know what that means." Gage struggled with the handcuffs and spreader bar. "Keep still! Why do they make these padlocks so damn small?" he complained.

Once Landry was free, Gage flopped onto his back pulling Landry on top of him. Landry did his best frog impression, spreading his arms and legs to cover as much of Gage's body as possible. They were both hot and sticky, but Landry didn't care. He needed close contact. He needed to know that he still had Gage's full attention.

Gage stroked his back and his ass, patting his hole with a finger. "Not too sore? I got a bit carried away."

"I like feeling you." Landry licked Gage's neck, enjoying the salty taste. "Both me and my butt are fine." He didn't resist as Gage lifted one of his hands and stroked his wrist.

"You're going to have marks here. I should use padded cuffs rather than the real deal."

"I like feeling them too," Landry said. "You know I do. I'd soon tell you if there was anything you did I didn't like. I have a safe word, remember?"

"I know you do, but I wouldn't hurt you for the world."

"Then do you mind not squeezing quite so hard. Can't breathe." Gage released his grip a fraction. Landry hummed his happiness, planting little kisses on Gage's chest. "I think you're getting hairier."

"Do you mind? I could always wax. I can't believe I said that."

"Tempting, but no. I love your fur. Maybe one day I'll get some too."

"You're so blond, it wouldn't show if you did. Besides I love you smooth."

"Feel so good. Warm and happy and..." Landry drifted into a doze and woke disoriented, still wrapped in Gage's arms. "What time is it?"

"A little after ten. You dropped off again."

"You should have woken me."

"You need the rest and besides, I like watching you sleep. I love the way you snuffle against me and rub your nose into my chest. It's very cute."

"You make me sound like a puppy."

"Not that cute."

Landry gasped in mock indignation. "I'm awake and hungry. We should shower. Can you call your friend in England today? I want to know what's going on with my portrait."

"Slow down! You may be awake but I'm still considering it." Gage yawned. "And you wish the portrait was yours! I wonder what it's worth."

"Millions, I guess. Hard to put a price on something like that. I suppose it'll go back to the family it was originally stolen from. It's pretty well documented where it came from, and there's an empty frame waiting for it in some museum."

"Well, we'll find out soon enough. Let's get clean, then I'll take you out for breakfast." Gage wound his fingers into Landry's hair, giving the strands gentle tugs. "I need bacon."

"You wanna come shower with me?" Landry felt strangely shy as he asked.

"Hmm, wet, soapy Landry seems like a good deal. Lead me to the bathroom, gorgeous."

Showering together lasted as long as the hot water did. Landry dropped to his knees and sucked Gage's dick until he was satisfied it was clean and shiny. Gage rewarded him with a little protein appetizer before breakfast then jacked Landry's cock while he fingered his hole, holding Landry up when his knees turned to jelly. Landry toweled down then dressed in a daze, soppy grin fixed to his face. He was so distracted he put on odd socks, one red and black stripes the other blue with yellow dots. He held out his feet, wiggled his toes and shrugged. "Petey is a trendsetter! Who knew?" He shoved his feet into an old pair of runners. He had dressed for comfort in soft jeans and a long-sleeved tee. Gage looked relaxed and comfortable in dark blue chinos and a pale blue polo shirt. Landry licked his lips and tried not to make his drooling too obvious—Gage was just as yummy dressed as he was naked.

Having decided on Basim's diner for breakfast, they strolled along the street hand-in-hand. Two guys were already hard at work repairing Treasure Trove's front door under the watchful eye of Mr. Lao, who must have opened the store's security shutters for them. Mr. Lao gave them a wave as they passed, and Landry promised to bring back a couple of waffles, which were Mr. Lao's biggest weakness.

Basim's place was packed because despite originating from Faisalabad and producing some amazing Pakistani cuisine thanks to his mom's recipes,

Basim cooked a mean American breakfast and everyone local knew it. His short stacks were legendary, and he'd managed to perfect the crispiest strips of bacon.

"This place is heaving, I'm not sure we're going to get in," Landry said, peering through the window.

Gage, who had a height advantage, waved at Basim from the doorway. Basim grinned and beckoned them over. Gage used his body to clear a path through the crowd, Landry tucked in behind him. Basim fingered the ends of his spectacular moustache. "Gage, Landry, it is madness in here this morning. The whole of Seattle needs Basim's pancakes. You want breakfast?"

"We do, but you seem to have the most popular diner in Seattle." Landry couldn't see a spare stool or table anywhere.

"For my friends, I find space. Follow me through to the kitchen." Basim found Landry and Gage a spot where two stools were pushed up against a prep counter a few feet away from where the kitchen staff were cooking up a storm. "Sit, relax. I'll bring you food."

Landry beamed. "You're the best, Basim. I'll say nice things about you to your mom next time I speak to her."

Basim bustled away but soon returned with miniature cups of potent coffee and a few minutes after that a procession of plates began arriving, seemingly carrying samples of virtually everything on the breakfast menu. Gage was in heaven, and Landry stole little bits of everything. "This has to be the best breakfast ever," Landry said, around a mouthful of syrup-soaked pancake.

"I'm gonna have to add half an hour to my workouts every day for the next month," Gage mumbled. "I don't care, it's worth it."

They ate steadily, with Basim's cooks insisting that they try new creations as well as their favorites. Landry finally pushed his plate away. "That's it, I can't eat another bite or I'll burst. Coffee now, that's a different matter. I wonder if there's a table free out front. I want to people watch and absorb caffeine."

Gage heaved himself off his stool. "Let's go see." He ordered coffee as they passed the counter where Basim and one of his staff were handling take-out orders. There was some space in the diner, and Gage snagged a corner booth next to the window thanks to a well-directed stare at the two chattering, twentysomethings who had the temerity to think they might get there first.

Landry settled into his seat feeling fat and contented. He patted his belly. "Can you check your messages? Now my brain isn't focused on food, I'm desperate to find out if there was anything down that well and if James Ellery is under lock and key. That would make my day."

"And mine. He wouldn't look good in a prison uniform." Gage grinned. He pulled out his cell and checked his messages. Landry fidgeted while Gage listened.

"Two from Sancha complaining about the amount of paperwork I create and one from London. DI Hughes asking me to call him back."

"What time is it in England?"

"Late afternoon, he'll still be at work."

"I want to hear what he says too. You can't put the phone on speaker in here so should we take our coffee to go?"

"Okay. Let's go back to the store."

Landry hopped from foot to foot while Gage arranged their take outs and paid for breakfast, insisting on giving Basim something even though he tried to wave Gage's money away.

"You really need some training in how to stay calm. This isn't going to help—I should have got you decaf." Gage thrust a cup of coffee into Landry's hand.

"You can spank me, tie me up, put me in chastity but forcing me to drink decaffeinated coffee is a step too far." Landry forgot to lower his voice and was overheard by several of Basim's patrons as Gage dragged him out onto the street.

"I think you've just traumatized some of Basim's regulars."

"You should be worried about my trauma," Landry exclaimed. "Unbelievable."

"Do you want me to make this call, or not?"

Landry scuffed his foot on the sidewalk. "Of course I do. Is that Petey, outside Treasure Trove?"

"It is."

Landry ran the last few yards to his friend. "Gage is going to ring his policeman friend in England and find out what happened at St. Cuthbert's. Wanna come and listen?"

"Yes!" Petey bounced with excitement. "I just swept the porch. The workmen are finished so I thought we may as well open. You can still have your day off, though. Mr. Lao said he'd be back later, and I can manage for a while. It seems a shame to close on such a nice day."

"And Carson's on shift so you've got nothing better to do," Landry said, laughing.

"I like to keep busy when he's not here. I lose my focus when he's not around and then get clumsy and drop things, but it doesn't seem to happen in the store. I think this place has an atmosphere of gravitas. It makes me responsible."

"If only it had the same effect on Landry," Gage said, joining them.

"Hey! Responsibility is way overrated. You're completely crazy, Petey, and that's why I love you." Landry followed Petey into the store. He and Petey shared the floral chaise longue while Gage sank into the leather club chair to make his call.

"Simon, it's Gage. You're on speaker. What news do you have for me?"

"Gage, how are things there in Seattle? I need to get over there for a visit."

"Not raining, so good thanks and you'd be welcome any time, my friend. How was your trip to the north yesterday?"

"Well, I've got good news and I've got bad news." Landry gripped Petey's hand. "The good news is that we did find something hidden down Cuddy's well as it's known locally and it was almost certainly a painting. The bad news is that the wrapping around it had disintegrated and the painting was little more than a soggy pile of mush. We'll get it tested to see if we can ascertain its age but if it was the *Portrait of a Young Man*, it's gone. With everything you told me about what you and Landry found, and the lengths someone went to to hide it, it could well have been the portrait. The canvas wrapping was certainly the right size."

Landry tried to hide his disappointment. Petey squeezed his fingers.

"That's a shame," Gage said. "It would have been amazing to find it intact, but I suppose it was always a long shot."

"We had to send one of our young coppers down the well. It took him a while, but he found a loose stone with a cavity hidden behind it. If he hadn't been specifically looking, and testing every stone, there's no way anyone else would have come across it by accident. Whoever used it as a hiding place, never intended for the treasure to be found by anyone not of their choosing."

"Well, it vindicates the search at least. I suppose it'll take a while to date the remains."

"The art world is not known for its speed," DI Hughes said. "I don't know if decayed, pulpy paper and paint is even datable, but I'll let you know as soon as I hear anything, one way or the other."

Landry poked Gage's arm. "What about Ellery?"

"Was there any sign of that guy I told you about, James Ellery?" Gage asked.

There was a moment's silence. Petey, Landry and Gage exchanged glances.

"Ah, yes, well... That's a little embarrassing."

"Spit it out, Simon. Did you get your hands on that slippery son of a bitch, or not?"

"We did and we didn't."

"He got away, didn't he?" Landry shouted.

"With hindsight," Inspector Hughes said, "I should have been more suspicious of a uniformed constable who happened to have climbing gear in the boot of his car. But, in my defense, young men have hobbies, don't they? We had asked the local station to send someone who could climb. He was blond, bearded, had a local accent and saved us a lot of time and effort by volunteering to go down the well. Said he was a member of the local mountain rescue team and had been asked to bring his gear along. But afterward, when I looked around to thank him, he'd disappeared. Turns out the local nick doesn't have any coppers by the name he gave me, and Mountain Rescue had never heard of him."

"Sounds just like the kind of thing he'd pull off," Gage said. "Though, he didn't have a beard when he was operating over here."

"Is there any way he could have brought something else out of the well without you seeing?" Landry asked.

"Absolutely not. He seemed pretty disappointed that he hadn't found anything more exciting than some pulpy scraps of paper."

"Thanks for telling us, Simon," Gage said. "We'd be very interested to hear any information on the paper when the boffins are finished with it. It was good to talk to you. If you ever need a favor in the future, you know where I am."

"Sure, mate. I'll talk to you soon. Bye."

"James Ellery is the sneakiest bastard I've ever come across," Gage said.

"He certainly has a set of cast-iron balls." Landry massaged his temples. "He must have been mightily annoyed not to find the portrait down that well. I take comfort in him having gotten wet and dirty at least."

"It must have been horrible down there," Petey said. "All dark and slimy. There were probably rats. And snakes."

"I'm not sure they have many snakes in England," Landry said. "Though James Ellery certainly qualifies. I can't believe he's added impersonating a police officer to his catalogue of crime. He's going to get away with it again, isn't he?"

Gage scowled. "Knowing him, yes. I wouldn't think Simon will want to waste resources on tracking him down."

"I guess it was always most likely that the portrait would be destroyed, but I kind of hoped it was intact. How wonderful if it had been preserved all these years and survived so many adventures."

"You're such a romantic." Gage leaned across and gave Landry a kiss. "And by the way, I don't want you thinking about that man's balls. Ever."

Petey snickered. "You're in big trouble now, Lan."

Landry eyed Gage. "Oh God, I hope so."

Chapter Eighteen

Four weeks later

Landry, Gage, Petey and Carson sat around a low table in a quiet corner of Scorch, well back from the dance floor where it was quiet enough to hold a conversation. A dozen plates containing a range of appetizers sat on the table. Carson was feeding Petey all his favorites while Gage and Landry were sharing some very garlicky prawns. Landry picked up a copy of the *Seattle Times* with greasy fingers. He'd brought it from home to show Petey, who hadn't seen it yet. "I still don't fucking believe it." He stared at the front page in disgust. It showed a picture of the *Portrait of a Young Man* alongside the beaming face of James Ellery. "'Astounding find.' Couldn't they have come up with a better headline than that? Something more accurate, like 'sneaky Brit steals old master'. He was on every news channel this morning too, and I got alerts on my cell. Lord help me!"

"I knew he'd found something when he sent me that text. 'Better luck next time.' The nerve of him. Damn it! There won't be a next time, if I ever get my hands on him." Gage scowled. "That man makes me want to get violent."

"Can I help?" Landry asked. "I could bring Petey's carpet beater."

"Yes, love. You can." Gage gave Landry a kiss.

"This was such a great plan, Gage," Petey said. "I hate that you and Landry didn't get the glory, so a commiseration celebration seems entirely fitting. After all the work you and Landry did to track down the Raphael, it's not fair. Yummy snacks make up for it, though."

"Love your priorities, honey." Carson slipped a slither of melon between Petey's lips.

"And James fucking Ellery gets all the credit," Landry said, stuffing a whole mozzarella stick in his mouth. "This entire article makes him out to be a hero. So magnanimous, gifting his find to the nation so that it can be returned to its rightful owner. Like he had any choice. Fuckety fuckety fuck!"

"He's unbelievable. He got exactly what he wanted — publicity. He's a master of spin. But we know the truth," Gage said. "The main thing is that the painting will go back to where it belongs and that it survived. That's a miracle in itself and some compensation, I suppose."

"How did he do it, though?" Carson asked. "Your DI friend was convinced he didn't bring anything else back up with him on the day they searched the well, wasn't he?"

"Simon, who's mad as hell by the way, thinks Ellery came prepared. Initial findings date the canvas and paper mush he produced to the right period. I'd say he took something he'd made down the well with him so he could 'discover' it. That meant that if he found the real thing, he could leave it there. It wouldn't have been difficult to go back again later. They thought they'd found what was left of the painting. There would have been no need for the British authorities to watch the well or go back for another look. We know he could climb and had the kit. Under cover of darkness in a rural place, no one would have spotted him. Simon told me that if Ellery has so much as an outstanding parking ticket, they'll be all over him like a very nasty, itchy crotch rash. His words, not mine, though I do like his thinking. I dearly hope they find something to pin on that bastard."

Carson snorted. "Fuck him. Who wants their face all over the papers anyway? We have good food and good company, Gage and Sancha are crime solving heroes thanks to closing the money laundering case, I got together with Petey because of that..." He sucked up a mark on Petey's neck. "And Landry, with a little bit of help from his friends, solved one of the greatest mysteries of our time. Not bad at all."

"We rock." Landry lifted his glass of juice in a toast. "To us." Everyone joined in the toast then Landry scrambled into Gage's lap "We are so lucky, and I guess Carson's right, I don't think I would have wanted all the attention that would have come with discovering the picture. We'd have had no privacy for ages and paparazzi would have been blocking the pavement outside the store. Mr. Lao wouldn't have liked that! It could have put off the customers." He wriggled. "Damn, these pants are tight."

"But they look fine." Gage laid his hand over Landry's rubber-covered crotch. "Sir!"

"Well, if you will dress to tempt me, what do you expect?"

"A little restraint in public?" Landry squeaked.

"Scorch is hardly public, Landry. Look around you." Gage chuckled. "And besides, I know damn well you love it. We're tame compared to what some people are getting up to in here." He tweaked the chain that ran from Landry's collar beneath the waistband of his pants where it was attached to a heavy cock ring.

Landry whimpered. "You are a bad, bad person. Tormenting poor little me when I've been good all day."

"You have an interesting definition of good."

"Good is me risking my manhood in these pants. It's not complaining about a cock ring that makes me hard but won't let me come. It's kneeling at your feet on a cushion that needed a whole 'nother duck's worth of feathers to make it comfortable — and just so we're clear I mean feathers that have been donated voluntarily." He nodded. "So there."

"So it wasn't you that snuck out to Krispy Kreme this morning, bought a box of donuts then ate three of them yourself?"

"No?" Landry blinked.

"Yes!" Petey and Carson shouted together.

"Traitors," Landry muttered. "Well yes, but I was hungry and I didn't eat all of them."

"Still, I think I'm entitled to a little bit of payback, don't you?" Gage played with the chain a little more.

"I saved one for you!"

"You ate the chocolate custard. That's my favorite. You know that but you ate it anyway. I see a great deal of chastity in your future, young man."

Landry sighed. "What's new? Like you even need an excuse to imprison my poor, defenseless dick."

Gage turned him over his knee, treating him to a very abrupt view of the floor. Half a dozen swift whacks to his ass followed. Gage lifted Landry back into place on his lap where Landry couldn't hide his grin or his burgeoning erection.

"You know that's not going to stop me eating the chocolate custard next time, don't you?" Landry shared a conspiratorial grin with Petey.

"Sadly, I do, but listen, I have news. A surprise," Gage said. "Not that a donut thief deserves it, but it's something to make up for the asshole-Brit-who-will-not-be-named."

Landry looked at him expectantly "I love surprises... Wait, is it the kind of surprise that ends up with me tied to the bed with something vibrating up my ass?"

"No." Gage rolled his eyes. "Not this time."

"Did you buy that sling you were looking at on the web the other day?" Landry bounced.

"Well yes, but that's not the surprise."

"So tell me! Do you know what's going on?" Landry accused Petey.

Petey shrugged. "Maybe?"

"So not fair!" Landry whined. "Why am I the only person who doesn't know the big secret?"

"If you stop talking for thirty seconds, I'd be able to tell you." Gage said.

"You could just gag him," Carson suggested, making Petey giggle and Landry pout. "Then you might get a word in."

"Give me strength." Gage gagged Landry's mouth with his hand. "Mr. Lao has an old friend who deals in coins and medals. He took the cross and the coin from the tin we found behind the waterfall and gave them to him for evaluation. It's taken a while because he needed to be sure, but it turns out that the coin is quite valuable. It's a rare one, worth around twenty thousand dollars."

"You're kidding!" Landry exclaimed. "That's brilliant. I thought it might be worth a few hundred dollars but hadn't gotten around to doing anything about it. But it doesn't belong to me, does it? I'll have to hand it in."

"Well, actually it does." Gage grinned. "You found it on public land, no one has ever lodged a claim for it as lost property and there are no records of that specific coin having been stolen—by the Nazis or by anyone else. I checked with one of the legal brains at work, and he said that abandoned property is property that the owner throws away or voluntarily forsakes its possession, and the first person to find it gets absolute title. Royston forsook, is that a word, possession of the tin, so it's yours just as much as if you'd found it in a mixed box from a yard sale. The same thing applies to the medal."

Landry gaped. "It's really mine? I've never owned anything that valuable in my life."

"And it's not the most valuable thing you own." Gage tousled Landry's hair. "Turns out the medal isn't a medal at all but would once have been a religious pendant. It's pure gold and the red stones that we assumed were glass are high-quality rubies." Landry grabbed his drink and took a long gulp. "A conservative estimate put its value at around two hundred thousand dollars," Gage said, "but rare religious artefacts can fetch huge sums at auction."

Landry put his glass down very carefully, hand shaking. He felt hot all over. Then he burst into tears.

Gage cuddled him close. "Why are you crying you daft thing?"

"I'm so happy," Landry managed to get out between sobs. "But I'm scared too. You'll help me decide what to do, won't you, Sir? I can't deal with this on my own."

"You'll never be on your own, love. Of course, I'll help. Mr. Lao's friend has potential buyers for both items already, if you decide you want to sell them. Mr. Lao is happy to negotiate on your behalf, and you know he'll get the best deal so there's nothing for you to worry about."

"He will," Landry said, relieved. "But all that money. I won't have earned it. It doesn't seem right."

"You wouldn't earn the money if you won the lottery," Petey said. "It's an amazing windfall and you'll be able to do lots of great things with it. There are plenty of charities you can donate to if you don't want to keep it all for yourself."

"I can't quite get my head around it," Landry said. "Help me, Sir?"

"How about we forget all about it for now and enjoy the evening. The four of us can have dinner together on Sunday and make a list of all the things you'd like to do with the money."

"Oh yes please! But the money must be for all of us. Finding the treasure was a joint effort, so everyone has to come with their own wish list."

Carson and Petey both protested but Gage hushed them. "If that's what Landry wants, that's what's gonna happen, so can it, you two."

"Honey, you're supposed to Dom me, not everyone else," Landry said. "But thank you. It'll be so much more fun if we're all involved. I'll make finger food and we can have pie!"

"I'm all in for pie," Carson said.

"I'll bring cookies," Petey contributed.

"Thank goodness that's settled." Gage rolled his eyes. "For now, I think my flogger arm is in need of exercise. Carson and I have reserved a private room for us to share. I called dibs on the St. Andrew's cross. I'm going to peel you out of those pants, Landry, strap you naked to the cross and make you forget your own name."

"I love you, Gage." A rush of relief and exhilaration coursed through Landry's body. "I know you'll always take care of me. You know exactly what I need even when I don't."

"And what you need right now is a flogging. I love you too, sweetheart. We should go get naked." Gage stood, throwing Landry over his shoulder.

"I think I just found some more treasure," Landry said, patting Gage's leather-wrapped ass. "Booty! That's another word for treasure, right?"

"Good Lord—get your hands off my booty. How about we stick to boring normality for a while," Gage said, marching across to the entrance to Scorch's private playrooms. "You've had enough adventures to last a lifetime."

"I wonder if anyone else would think our normality is boring," Landry giggled, waving to Petey who was following behind hand-in-hand with Carson.

"All I'm saying is that Carson and I would appreciate it if the pair of you kept yourselves out of trouble for a while," Gage muttered, setting Landry on his feet. "No hidden treasure, no gang violence and absolutely no consorting with British criminals."

"Just chains, canes and chastity, huh?"

"Yes, my beautiful brat. Exactly that."

Want to see more from this author? Here's a taster for you to enjoy!

Treasure Trove Antiques: The Poison Bottle
L.M. Somerton

Excerpt

Landry Carran gave his ass a rub and grinned at the resulting ache. His boyfriend and Dom, Detective Gage Roskam had delivered a stupendous spanking less than an hour earlier, and Landry was still glowing, physically and mentally. He gave a happy jig then bounced down the stairs from the apartment he shared with Gage to Treasure Trove Antiques, which occupied the ground floor of the building and was his place of gainful-ish employment. Two cups of strong coffee and a bowl of sugar-laden cereal ensured his current energetic state would last for at least an hour, which was when his best friend and assistant, Petey Templeton, would join him. Landry didn't usually have to open the store alone, but Petey had finally given in to a nagging toothache and had an early dental appointment.

"Such a wuss," Landry muttered. "Can't believe I had to bribe him to go." *Worth it though. An assistant who doesn't want to eat baked goods is no use to me at all. That globe he had his eye on was a small price to pay.*

Petey had a thing for maps and had fallen in love with a battered globe that dated to the nineteen seventies and was about as accurate as a Fox News report. Landry had gotten so fed up of Petey whining about his tooth, he'd promised Petey the globe if he got it sorted. Landry had also persuaded Carson, Petey's boyfriend, to act as escort and make sure he made his appointment. Carson had been happy to help out because, as he'd put it, 'a boyfriend who cries when you kiss him does not boost a man's confidence'.

Bopping and humming as he went, Landry unlocked the door between the stairwell and the store. As he entered the cavernous space, piled high with antiques and collectables, he took a deep breath. The familiar scent of beeswax polish, old wood and leather always settled him and put him in the right frame of mind for a day at work.

He moved around the store turning on an eclectic mix of lighting—mainly old lamps that were for sale because his boss, Mr Lau, insisted that they were more attractive to potential buyers when lit. Of course that meant that whenever they sold one, a corner of the store would get dark until a new one was sought to replace it, but Landry didn't mind because part of Treasure Trove Antiques' charm was its nooks and crannies.

He knew the stock back to front but loved seeing the wonder on customers' faces when they spotted something unique or unusual hidden behind an ageing armoire or balancing on top of a bookcase stuffed with rare tomes. He glanced around, checking that all was as he'd left it the previous evening. Everything was as it should be.

Not that there was any reason for him to think otherwise, but there had been an incident with a mouse once when somehow, the tiny rodent had set up home in a basket of vintage tablecloths and had nibbled a hole through two of them before he was spotted. It had taken a humane trap and enough peanut butter to feed a raccoon, let alone a mouse, to catch the beast so Landry was constantly on the lookout for any signs of critters in the store.

He grabbed the long pole he needed to push the security shutter into place then went back into the hall. He left the building then crossed the yard to the alley gate. After his usual fight with the padlock, he rounded the corner of the building to the street. His friend Priya, whose dad owned the Eastern Emporium opposite Treasure Trove, was outside brushing down the sidewalk with hot soapy water. Landry gave her a wave before jogging across the road.

"What's going down?"

"What came up, more like." She grimaced. "Somebody deposited the contents of their stomach on the sidewalk last night. So gross."

Landry wrinkled his nose. "Rather you than me."

"Hey, if you wanna do a girl a favour, I'd be happy to hand over the broom."

"No can do." Landry grinned. "Petey's at the dentist so I have to open on my own this morning. Gotta go before hordes of ravening customers start beating on the security shutter."

"Yeah, I can see where they're lining up around the block." Priya resumed brushing. "I'll come over on my break later. You can buy me a coffee."

"Deal. Have a good morning." Landry skipped back across the street, managing not to trip over his pole. He had less trouble opening the security shutter than closing it because he didn't have to get the hook on the end of his pole through the tiny D-ring that allowed him to draw them down. It was way above his head and like trying to thread a needle while standing on the deck of a pitching boat. Opening up just meant using the pole to push the shutter into place once he'd released the padlock that locked to a concealed ring in the sidewalk.

A padlock that's no longer in place.

Landry frowned. He distinctly remembered locking it the night before because he'd scraped a knuckle doing it. "Fuckety fuck. What the heck is going on?"

There was no sign of vandalism or any other damage to the shutter. Landry shrugged, slipped the pole into place then pushed. The shutter rolled up of its own accord, only needing another shove for the last couple of feet. Landry unhooked the pole then gaped. In the recessed store doorway, was a person, huddled in a ball, facing away from him.

"What on earth...? Hey, you can't stay there." He groped in his pocket for a few dollars. "Go get some breakfast."

Whoever it was didn't move. With a sick feeling in the pit of his stomach, Landry propped his pole against the store window then leaned over his visitor. He touched his shoulder, gave it a little shake, and the man rolled toward him.

"Holy fuck!" *He's dead!* The front of the beige trench coat he wore was stained with blood. There was a blue tinge to his skin and his eyes were open, staring.

Landry danced back a few steps as he stared at the corpse. "No, no, no... This is not good for business. I mean, poor guy but why *my* shop doorway?" His cell was inside so he turned and waved frantically at Priya who dropped her brush before running across the street. "Call 911! I found a body."

Priya, who was always good in a crisis, did an about turn and rocketed into the Eastern Emporium. She soon returned with her dad at her side.

"The cops are on their way," she said, putting an arm round Landry's now shaking shoulders. "You should call Gage. Here, use this." She handed over her cell, but Landry's hands were trembling too much to dial the number. Priya grabbed it . "Tell me the number."

Landry reeled it off without thinking. He couldn't tear his eyes away from the dead body.

"Gage, its Priya. I'm here with Landry and… Yes, he's fine but the dead guy he just found behind the security shutter isn't so good."

"What?" Landry heard Gage's yell even from where he was standing. He took the phone back.

"Can you come home, Sir?" Landry used the honorific without thinking, defaulting to his role as Gage's submissive rather than his boyfriend in his stressed state. "There's a bbb…body. A real-life body, I mean it's a dead body but it's real. An actual genuine, honest to God, not breathing, corpse. And it's in the shop porch blocking the door and there's blood. Gage, why is there a dead person in my shop doorway?" Tears welled in Landry's eyes, and he sniffled.

"Stay put. Sancha and I are on our way. Who's there with you?"

"Petey's at the dentist and Mr Lao isn't here, but Priya and her dad have come over."

"Stay with them. I mean it, Landry. You are not to go anywhere on your own."

"Not going anywhere," Landry mumbled as Gage ended the call. "How can I go anywhere when there is a dead person?"

Priya gave him a comforting hug. She and her dad had been joined by the guy who had been cleaning windows at the café next door and the crew of a passing garbage truck. The manager of the café arrived with a tray of coffees and a plate piled with Danish pastries.

"I know it doesn't seem appropriate," she said, "but a hot drink and something sweet will take your mind off what's going on, Landry. It'll help with the shock."

"Thanks Mary." Landry discovered that shoving a cherry Danish in his mouth made all the difference. A new infusion of sugar and caffeine into his system helped him see things in a more clinical light and stop thinking about how on earth a dead guy had gotten behind the security shutter.

"The padlock," he said, spraying crumbs. "When I came to lift the shutter earlier, the padlock was gone. I wonder where it is."

The small crowd started searching up and down the sidewalk and it wasn't long before there was a shout from one of the garbage crew. "Found it!" Landry, coffee in hand, walked over to take a look at where the guy was pointing. The padlock lay in the gutter, partly covered by a discarded banana skin.

"I guess we should leave it where it is," Landry said, "in case of fingerprints."

"That's right. I'm Elton." The garbage guy held out his hand, which Landry shook, hoping that his fingers wouldn't get crushed in the process. Elton was built like a line-backer.

"Nice to meet you, Elton. Shame it couldn't have been under better circumstances."

"You'd be surprised how many bodies we come across in our line of work," Elton said, sounding philosophical. "We get training on what not to do when it comes to possible evidence. We were about to empty the dumpsters along the street when we saw what was going on, so we'll leave them until the cops get here. They may want to keep the contents to search for clues."

"Well, I never thought of that."

"I don't suppose antique selling is a job that gets you involved in much crime," Elton said.

Landry thought about the last few months, the adventures he and Gage had had first with his lucky cat and then the gilded mirror. "No, not really."

"I wonder if there are any pastries left." Elton ambled toward the café where Mary was eyeing him like a piece of prime beef. Landry shook his head. "People sure do meet under the strangest of circumstances."

Sirens announced the arrival of the cops and not long afterward, Gage's Jeep screeched to a halt next to a patrol car. He and Sancha jumped out and while Sancha went over to the uniforms, Gage headed straight for Landry.

"Again? Really?" He drew Landry into a tight hug.

"So not my fault," Landry muttered against the hard planes of Gage's chest. "It's not like I have a sign up saying leave your dead bodies here, is it?"

"You attract trouble like a magnet."

Landry nuzzled against Gage's body. He could feel the warmth of his skin through his shirt and smell the lemony stuff he'd used in the shower that morning. "Do not."

"Do so."

"Someone cut off the padlock, it's in the gutter over there. They must have lifted the grill, dumped the body in the porch then pulled it down again."

"I want you to go sit in the café," Gage said, "while Sancha and I get things started."

"Will you be assigned the case?" Landry asked.

"If the captain doesn't think I have a conflict-of-interest, it's quite likely." Gage steered Landry toward the café. He gestured at Priya and asked her to stay with Landry.

Landry didn't want to leave the safety of Gage's arms but knew he had to let him do his job. Once he was settled at a table in the café with Priya next to him, he took a deep breath and eased some of his tension with a roll of his shoulders.

He took a long swig of coffee. "Here we go again."

"Are you ready for another adventure?" Priya asked.

"It's not like I had a choice the first time, or the second. Hopefully this will amount to nothing." Landry didn't need Priya's sceptical expression or his own gut feeling to tell him that amounting to nothing was the least likely outcome of the morning's events. He wondered if impending doom merited another pastry.

About the Author

Lucinda lives in a small village in the English countryside, surrounded by rolling hills, cows and sheep. She started writing to fill time between jobs and is now firmly and unashamedly addicted.

She loves the English weather, especially the rain, and adores a thunderstorm. She loves good food, warm company and a crackling fire. She's fascinated by the psychology of relationships, especially between men, and her stories contain some subtle (and some not so subtle) leanings towards BDSM.

L.M. Somerton loves to hear from readers. You can find her contact information, website details and author profile page at https://www.pride-publishing.com